M

'Let me give

Olivia nodded at

'Break up with h

'Pardon?'

'Whoever he is. Just dump him. You clearly don't have eyes only for him—which suggests to me that you're wasting your time. No woman should be prepared to settle for second-best. And one as pretty as you certainly shouldn't need to!'

Olivia felt her skin burn. How she hated Leon's arrogant assumption!

Dear Reader

The first few months of a new year are a time for looking forward and wondering what the future holds for us. There are no such worries when you pick up a Mills & Boon story, though—you're guaranteed to find an exciting, heart-warming romance! This month, as usual, we've got some real treats in store for you. So, whatever 1995 brings you, you can be sure of one thing: if you're reading Mills & Boon, it's going to be a year of romance!

The Editor

Jenny Cartwright was born and raised in Wales. After three years at university in Kent and a year spent in America, she returned to Wales where she has lived and worked ever since. Happily married with three young children—a girl and two boys—she began to indulge her lifelong desire to write when her lively twins were very small. The peaceful solitude she enjoys while creating her romances contrasts happily with the often hectic bustle of her family life.

Recent titles by the same author:

BLAMELESS DESIRE
PASSIONATE OPPONENT
FORSAKING ALL REASON

TEMPTATION
ON TRIAL

BY
JENNY CARTWRIGHT

MILLS & BOON

MILLS & BOON LIMITED
ETON HOUSE, 18-24 PARADISE ROAD
RICHMOND, SURREY TW9 1SR

*MILLS & BOON and the Rose Device
are trademarks of the publisher.*

*First published in Great Britain 1995
by Mills & Boon Limited*

© Jenny Cartwright 1995

*Australian copyright 1995   Philippine copyright 1995
This edition 1995*

ISBN 0 263 78899 7

*Set in Times Roman 10 on 11½ pt.
01-9503-55017 C*

Made and printed in Great Britain

CHAPTER ONE

LIVVY wished she had an anatomy textbook with her. When he lifted the axe, two broad muscles rippled into view, hard and powerful, and then disappeared as the bright blade swung through the hazy morning sunshine and bit into the pale wood. She wished now that she had paid more attention at college. Which muscles were they, and would she be able to identify them when she got back home and was able to look them up? She patted the pockets of her crisp blue and white striped sundress, although she knew already that no pencil and paper lurked there ready to record the image.

His back was an anatomical masterpiece, she decided, so broad, the bones obviously big and hard and well-formed, the indentation of his spine so graceful. His skin shone with sweat, a golden-brown, lustrous where the sun bathed him most brilliantly, beneath his nape, across the expanse of his shoulders, a darker bronze in the hollow of his back. When he raised the heavy axe she saw that the rich hue of his sunburnt forearms was muted by dark, curling hairs. She visualised herself dragging the side of a pencil flat against a sheet of grainy paper to achieve the rough, textured effect of male hair on skin, and shivered with pleasure.

He straightened up, having obviously done as much damage to the tree stump as he needed to do, dropped the axe into the wet grass and laid the palms of his hands flat against the small of his back, his fingertips tucking into the waistband of his black jeans as he eased the tension out of his big frame. Then he picked up the axe, swung it casually up on to his shoulder and pushed it back, so that the glinting steel lay for a brief moment close against his sinewy neck. Then he turned.

Livvy hastily looked away and hurried on up the pathway towards the house. She would have to ask Major Fox why he'd had that tree felled. It was a wonderful old tree and had looked perfectly healthy to her, but older people, especially people like Major Fox, often weren't conscious that in this day and age it just wasn't acceptable to chop down trees without having sound ecological reasons for doing so. Though perhaps she wouldn't comment on the tree; or at least not until she'd asked her favour of him... It would be crazy to go upsetting the man at this stage.

As it happened it took longer to reach the house than she'd anticipated. Bright, new chainlink fencing sliced across the pathway and she was forced to turn back and go round via the road after all. Drat. That was another thing she ought to speak to Major Fox about. The path was a public right of way—everyone knew that.

But by the time she reached the cobbled courtyard in front of the old, half-timbered building the sunshine and birdsong had soothed away her indignation. She felt blissfully happy, and consequently found herself yanking on the bell-pull with rather more exuberance than she had intended. The bells rang and rang, gradually dying away to no more than an echo as she waited. After what seemed like an age, the door swung open abruptly with a wild, yowling squeak that would have done credit to a third-rate horror movie.

'Um...hello.'

He had a white towel around his neck and a large white T-shirt was concealing the hairs on his chest and the hard wall of his abdomen. She recognised the hair of his head, though. Those almost sculpturally perfect, heavy black curls were too distinctive to forget.

He didn't speak. he just fixed his surprisingly blue eyes on her face and looked at her.

'Um... I was wondering if I could see Major Fox.'

He still didn't say anything. One eyebrow curved upwards quizzically, but that was all.

'I haven't got an appointment. I mean, he's not expecting me or anything. But...um...I do know him.'

'Not very well, though.'

The voice was as dark as his hair. So where on earth did he get those blue eyes from? They were totally unexpected, set as they were in a face that was almost Middle-Eastern in it's strong lines and graceful planes.

'Uh... no. I don't know him very well. He is all right, though, isn't he? I mean, there's not something I ought to know, is there?'

Now the other eyebrow quirked upwards, and the heavy eyelids, edged with long black lashes, lowered marginally to complete the air of sardonic amusement.

'He's still alive, if that's what's worrying you,' came the laconic reply.

'Oh. Good.'

His eyebrows didn't budge. He didn't say anything further.

'Is he—er—is he well?'

A faint hint of a nod settled that question.

'Look, isn't he here? Is that the problem? Because if he's not here then perhaps I could see Mrs Major Fox or leave a message or something.'

'Mrs Major Fox?'

'Yes,' explained Livvy hurriedly, unnerved by the man's taciturnity. 'I used to know her when I was a child. That's what I used to call her then and...um...it just slipped out. You see, my grandparents used to live in the village, but they've retired to Worthing—they've got a bungalow there because my grandmother has an arthritic hip—so I haven't been here for some years, but I used to know the Foxes years ago and they always exchange Christmas cards with my grandparents, so I just thought I'd look in and...uh...' She stopped. Why the hell was she telling him all this? 'Look, aren't they here?'

'No.'

'Oh. Have they moved?'

'Yes.'

'I see. Have they gone far?'

'To Darjeeling.'

'Oh. Good grief!'

Now one corner of his mouth joined in the smile. It was a bit like watching a slow-motion action replay of a smile, so tiny were the movements of his facial muscles. She remembered the swift play of light on the surface of his mobile back as he swung the axe and bent to scoop shards of wood from the centre of the stump. He could move fast enough when it suited him.

'When did they go?' she continued irritably, wishing she weren't so transfixed by his physical attributes.

'Last week.'

'Drat.'

Livvy bit down on her generous lower lip and frowned. She had meant to come the weekend before last but her parents had left her in charge of the shop. Oh, damn and blast—why did she let them impose on her all the time? 'I presume ... I mean, have *you* bought the house from them?'

He gave another of his minimal nods, his eyes still locked lazily on to her face.

'Then you'll have a forwarding address. Do you think I could trouble you for it? I do need to get in touch with him fairly quickly.'

'Come in. I'll see if I can find it for you.'

Livvy shivered. She thought she'd pass on that one. She was already sick and tired of her inability to take her eyes off this man's exceptional physique. 'Um...if you don't mind...I'm in a hurry. I'll wait on the step.'

'What's the urgency?'

'Oh. I'm very busy. You know. I have to get back.'

'But I thought you said you were just passing and you thought you'd stop by?'

'I didn't actually say that I was just passing. As it happens I've just driven here from Bristol specifically to see Major Fox on a business matter, Mr...Um?'

'Roche. Leon Roche.' Both his face and his eyes hardened slightly as he introduced himself.

'Olivia Houndsworth,' she responded briskly. 'Pleased to meet you, Mr Roche.'

And then he raised one large, sun-browned hand and offered it to her. She took it, surprised to find the skin of his palm dry and smooth and decidedly uncalloused. Having watched him wielding the axe, she had gained an impression of a body work-hardened in every respect. His grip was firm and strong, pleasing, at first, though to her consternation the pressure began to increase perceptibly as she left her fingers in his. She drew her own long-fingered hand away sharply, and nursed it to her chest.

'What's the matter? Did it hurt?' His smile, such as it was, was back in place.

'Not exactly,' she returned acerbically, meeting his gaze determinedly with her own large, mossy-green eyes. 'But I suspect it might have done had I left my hand there much longer.'

He just raised his eyebrows a notch higher and stared. There was nothing apologetic in his scrutiny. In fact, had he been much younger than the thirty-five or so years his appearance suggested, she would have thought his expression insolent.

Flustered, Livvy used her right hand to push her long, auburn hair back from her face. 'Are you able to give me the address, Mr Roche?'

'Yes.'

'Good. Because I'm in a hurry and——'

'No, you're not.'

'I beg your pardon?'

One corner of his mouth curled upwards scornfully. 'You can't possibly be in a hurry. You have just discovered that you have available the time you were planning to spend talking business with the major. Unless you're planning a mad dash from the nearest airport to India to catch him before lunch, you cannot possibly be in a hurry.'

'No. Well.' Livvy pressed her full lips tight together and made another unnecessary sortie into the heavy mass of her hair with her long, slender fingers. 'I have other things to do, actually.'

Now he gave a full-blooded smile, his mouth breaking open, his teeth very white against the dark shadow of his unshaven chin. But he didn't say anything.

'Oh!' exclaimed Livvy, exasperated by his silence. 'Could I have that address, please? Then I can go.'

He stood back and gestured her inside with one hand.

Despite his casual appearance there was a distinct air of command about the man when he stirred himself, which had her jumping unquestioningly to obey him. 'Into the wolf's lair I go,' she muttered drily to herself as she stepped over the uneven lintel and into the gloom of the hall.

'Do you think I'm a wolf?' he asked with unnerving directness.

He wasn't supposed to have heard that! 'Oh. No. Of course not.'

'Why did you say what you said, then?'

'I...um... Look, Mr Roche, I'm not sure that I want to be inside your house. I mean, I don't know you from Adam. That's why I said it.'

He narrowed his eyes and broadened his smile. 'You're quite safe, Miss Houndsworth. I don't bite.'

'Good...' She sighed, longing to be back out in the sunshine.

Leon Roche turned his back on her and strolled across the dark, panelled hall to the massive chimney-piece, in front of which had been pushed a modern office desk made of utilitarian steel, lacquered grey, its top littered with papers—and no fewer than three telephones. Her eyes followed him—until she put one hand to her brow and rubbed irritably, trying to erase the image of his naked shoulders which was busily painting itself in her mind, superimposing itself on the blank canvas of the white T-shirt. He had the wrong colouring and the wrong sort of build for the man she needed to draw, anyway.

At last she dropped her hand, looking purposefully upwards at the chimney-breast, refusing to allow herself to study him any longer.

'Oh!' she found herself exclaiming. 'You've got the major's head.'

He looked up from the papers he was sifting through and glanced at her over his shoulder, a wry smile of disbelief in place.

'I didn't mean that you look like him! Anyway, he's bald... No. I meant the antelope's head up there. The stuffed one. Over the mantelpiece. It's his. He was very proud of it.'

Leon turned back to face her, a small crocodile bound personal organiser and a gold pen held loosely in one hand. 'Was he? I can't imagine why. It's horrible.'

'Isn't it? I hate stuffed animals personally. They simply exist to glorify the hunt, don't they?' God, the man was absolutely *beautiful*. It wasn't just the muscles and the curls and the features; it was the way he held himself— the way he moved. Everything. 'They're grisly, don't you think?'

He looked her up and down very slowly at that point. The hall was large and there was some considerable distance between them, so it was very obvious what he was doing. His hooded blue eyes skimmed first the top of her head, following the line of her long, twisting mane of shiny hair to her shoulders, then down over her breasts, past her waist and the rounded curve of her hips till he reached her toes peeping out from her pretty leather sandals. Then they travelled up again to settle on her face. 'So *you* don't go hunting, Miss Houndsworth?' he said at length, his voice low and gravelly and disparaging. 'You do surprise me.'

'No,' she replied, disconcerted.

His eyes cooled almost tangibly, but his mouth flickered again as if hinting at a smile.

'Why does it surprise you?'

He didn't reply.

'I mean, most people don't go hunting, do they?' she continued, trying to make her earlier comment seem rhetorical. 'And I'm not wearing jodhpurs or anything, so I don't understand why it should surprise you.'

His eyes narrowed again. 'From the way you were looking at me when I was hacking out that tree stump I got the impression that you might not be averse to the chase, Miss Houndsworth.'

Livvy felt a fierce blush sweep over her high cheek-bones. She blinked fast. 'You had your back to me,' she accused.

He crooked one eyebrow. 'Yes. But I knew you were there, all the same. I saw you approaching from a distance, and then I could see your feet and legs every time I bent down to clear away the chips. You were watching me for quite a while.'

'Only for technical reasons,' she returned stiffly. 'I was surveying you in connection with my work.'

He let out an abrupt burst of laughter. 'Where's the theodolite?'

Livvy cleared her throat. 'I'm an illustrator. I'm at present working on an illustration of a man. I was interested in certain anatomical details. That's all.'

One eyebrow flickered. 'So you want me to sit for you?'

'No! Good gracious, no. I mean, it was just the muscle groups of the shoulders. I can look it up in a textbook, actually.'

He laid one square-tipped finger across his lips. The gesture didn't even begin to disguise his scornful amusement. With the other hand he held out the book and pen to her. 'The address is in here. Under F for Fox. There's a tear-off pad inside the front cover. You can use that to copy it down.'

Livvy sensed the challenge implicit in his invitation. He wanted her to come towards him and take it from him. She was to be the one to make a move... 'Can't you copy it out for me?' she returned thornily. 'I don't like going through people's private papers.'

There was a contemptuous pause. 'You have my consent.'

She took a deep breath and walked over to him, almost snatching the book from his hand. Then she moved to the corner of the desk and placed the book on it, letting her long hair swing over her shoulder to conceal her face as she turned the pages.

His handwriting was big and bold and difficult to decipher. Everything was written in the same black ink which flowed from the gold nib of his pen as she hastily copied down the major's address in the Himalayas. With relief she pocketed the slip of paper and swung around to face the open door. 'Thank you, Mr Roche,' she said coolly, stepping boldly towards the sunshine and fresh air. 'I'm sorry to have disturbed you.'

'Liar.'

The single softly spoken word caught her ear at exactly the same moment as the hall-stand caught her eye. She halted in the doorway, dithering. God, but it peeved her to have to turn back and ask him yet another question, but there was no way around it. She tossed her hair back over her shoulders and half turned. 'I notice you still have some of the major's bits and pieces.'

'Yes.'

Oh, what was the matter with him? Why couldn't he talk like everybody else?

'Many?'

'Yes.'

'Well, could you reassure me that he has taken the contents of the library with him?'

'No.'

Infuriated, Livvy ran both sets of fingers through her hair, throwing it back from her high forehead and surveying him haughtily over her flushed cheekbones. 'Could you enlighten me a little further, Mr Roche? Does that mean that the contents of his library are intact or not?'

He was leaning back against the desk now, his buttocks propped against the edge, his feet, clad in grey leather boots, crossed at the ankle. 'It means that he and his wife have left most of the contents of the house here. I was obliged to pay a premium price for a cardboard box full of old dusters in the scullery and a trunk full of ancient corsets, among other things. It appears that I also now own the contents of the library—though the major did arrange for a number of packing cases to be collected a day or so after I moved in. I believe they may have contained some private books and papers—in fact, I'm sure that they did. But the library itself seems to have been left more or less undisturbed. Does that answer your question, Miss Houndsworth?'

She sighed, letting her hands fall limply to her sides. 'Unfortunately, yes,' she muttered. 'In which case it seems that I did not call here to discuss a business matter with Major Fox. I called here to discuss a business matter with you, Mr Roche. Do you think you could possibly spare me a little of your time?'

He tilted his head slightly to one side and surveyed her steadily. Then another broad smile broke across his face, like a wave on the sand. 'By all means,' he said. 'However, although I admire the blind optimism which brought you haring up here from Bristol first thing on a Saturday morning without ringing first to check that you'd be welcome, I'm afraid I don't conduct my own affairs quite so inefficiently. When you rang the doorbell I was on my way to take a shower prior to keeping a ten o'clock appointment in Hereford.' He glanced at the Rolex on his wrist. 'I can spare you seven minutes and a cup of coffee. Will that be sufficient?'

Seven Minutes? 'Plenty. And we can skip the coffee.'

He turned his back on her and began sauntering across the hall and through one of the doors leading off.

She stood there bleakly for a minute, watching him disappear. It was quite obvious that she was expected to follow him—and if she didn't he certainly wouldn't come looking for her. Her seven minutes were ticking by. She clenched her fists and followed him, catching up with him as he led the way down a long passage to a surprisingly modern all-white kitchen. Once there he flicked the switch on the automatic jug kettle, extracted one mug and a jar of instant coffee from a cupboard, and stuck his hand in the fridge and produced a pint of milk. He didn't look at her and he didn't speak.

'The thing is, Mr Roche,' she began when she had finally caught hold of her annoyance, screwed it into a tiny knot, and tucked it away where it could do no harm, 'I was wondering if I could go through the library and see if I can find something. I'm looking for a document that Major Fox showed me some years ago. I need to see it in connection with my work.'

He shook a little coffee into the mug without using a spoon, added boiling water and milk and sat down on one of the white chairs at the white table. He sipped slowly and then set the mug in front of him. 'I thought you said you were an illustrator?'

'I am.'

He shrugged his shoulders slightly, looking into her eyes. 'I fail to see an obvious connection. Enlighten me.'

Livvy sighed heavily. 'It's a long story, Mr Roche,' she said, biting on the inside of her lip.

'Then you won't be able to explain it to me right now, will you?'

She pulled a rueful, pleading face. 'No. But—oh, all I want to do is look through the stuff in the library. Surely it won't matter to you? It's not as if the document has any relevance to you at all.'

He glanced at his watch again. Then he laid his finger across his full lower lip and surveyed her. 'Why not put it in writing? I can consider your request at my leisure then. And perhaps get my solicitor to have a look at your proposal.'

'Solicitor? Look, I fail to see why you're being so obtuse about this. The piece of paper in question is a sort of story—a handwritten record made by a villager about a hundred and fifty years ago. It's just a tale. The thing is that I'm illustrating the story and I need to see the original.' She shook her head in frustration. 'Can't you give me an answer now? Do you have to get a solicitor to look into it?'

He took another sip of his coffee then ran the tip of his tongue across his lower lip. 'Yes,' he said briskly, standing up.

'But why?'

'I can think of a variety of legal problems off the top of my head. Ownership. Consent. Copyright.' He glanced at his watch again. 'Now if you don't mind...?' And he began making his way towards the door, the mug in his hand. He stood back, waiting for her to precede him out of the room.

Haughtily she made her way back to the hall, taking great care not to brush against him as she passed through the kitchen door. Once out in the sunshine she took even greater care not to look back. She was seething.

And she had plenty of time to seethe before she reached her car, not being able to use the footpath as a short cut. Oh, damn it. Why hadn't she come the weekend before last? Why had she just caved in when her mother and father had requested a ten-minute break while they popped off to select a bathroom suite? It wasn't even as if it was essential. For a one-bathroom family they had spent an unconscionable amount over the years on low-level cisterns in an array of fashionable colours. Halfway back to the pub car park where she'd left her battered Mini he swooped past her in something unidentifiable, petrel-blue, low-slung, foreign and fast. He screeched to a halt a few yards in front of her and opened the passenger door. 'Get in,' he said. 'I'll give you a lift.' He was wearing a navy suit with a blue shirt. His curls were still damp, and his chin shone from the assault of the razor. Now he looked formidably austere, and smelt faintly of an expensive, woody aftershave.

'No, thanks. It's a beautiful morning and I'm enjoying the fresh country air.'

He frowned exasperatedly. 'Don't be stubborn. We're miles from anywhere and you're wearing a very flimsy pair of high-heeled shoes. Get in. Unless you actually enjoy having blisters.'

Once again she found herself doing as she was told, but at least she did it with an angry flounce. The seats in the machine were absurdly low and absurdly deep. Once she had fastened her seatbelt and was pinned back against the leather upholstery she felt diminutive and powerless, like a child on a fairground ride, especially when the car surged noiselessly into life again.

'I'm parked in the car park of the Boar's Head.'

'Why didn't you drive right up to Purten End?'

'I love the countryside. It's a beautiful morning and I fancied the walk—except that the footpath had been fenced off and I had to turn back and use the road.'

'Yes. I know. I had it done.'

'Don't you realise that the path is a public right of way?'

'So I've been told,' he replied dismissively.

'Well, surely you realise that you can't just block off footpaths like that? If I were you I'd consult that solicitor of yours about it.'

He gave another of his short, rich laughs at that, leaving her feeling stung.

'Or perhaps I shall consult my solicitor about it,' she said primly.

'Do you have one?'

'The Ramblers' Association does, I'm sure,' she returned triumphantly. 'I'm sure it will be very interesting, Mr Roche.'

And then he took his eyes off the road for a fleeting moment and flashed her a very dangerous look from eyes which were the coldest of Antarctic blues she had ever seen. 'Just leave it alone, Miss Houndsworth, eh? You'll never again have occasion to use that footpath, so it would be absurd wasting any of your precious time on the matter. I'm sure the local people will do what is necessary if they find it an inconvenience.'

She glared at him, though it was pretty pointless as his eyes were now back on the winding lane ahead of them. 'Does that mean you don't intend letting me search through your library?'

He sighed. 'I'm having the house cleared very shortly. I doubt it will be possible. However, as I said earlier, if you care to put the matter in writing I shall ensure that it gets the consideration it deserves.'

Livvy screwed up her fists. 'Mr Roche, I do think you should know that it's terribly, awfully important to me that I see that document again. My career sort of depends on it, in fact. You see, I'm halfway through the book already and I can't get any further without it and my agent isn't being very friendly and I'll have to do the gardening book he wants me to do otherwise, and I'll lose my chance with the publishers if I don't finish it in six months.'

'Then you'd better make it a good letter, hadn't you?'

She screwed up her face and closed her eyes tight shut, and then opened them very wide. 'What did I do wrong? Why don't you like me?'

She saw that sardonic amusement move the muscles of his face almost imperceptibly yet again. 'Whatever gives you the idea that I don't like you?'

'Oh, come on. I'm not a fool. You *don't* like me, do you?'

'Miss Houndsworth, I don't know you. Consequently I can hardly claim to dislike you.'

'It's quite possible to dislike someone at first sight. Is that what happened?'

'Like love at first sight?'

'If you like.'

'I don't believe in love at first sight, Miss Houndsworth.'

'So what? We're talking here about dislike at first sight, and that definitely exists whether you believe in it or not. I know because I've actually disliked people on sight myself. Quite a lot of times, actually, though I'm not proud of the fact.'

'You didn't dislike me at first sight,' he said with a distinct air of certainty.

'Er... Well, no. But the question is, did you dislike *me* at first sight?'

'No.'

'So what did I do wrong?'

'You really want to know?'

'I think I'd better. It's very important to me. My whole future could depend on knowing.'

He didn't reply. Well...she was already getting used to that. He swung the big car into the pub car park and pulled up alongside her battered Mini, which was the only other car there so early in the morning. Then he leaned across her and opened her door.

Her stomach lurched. Bits of his jacket were brushing across her flesh, making her skin hum with awareness. She turned her muddled green eyes pleadingly towards him one last time as she unfastened her belt and scrambled out. He reached across her seat again to shut the door, and looked very hard into her eyes. 'Let me give you a piece of advice,' he said coolly.

She nodded attentively.

'Break up with him.'

'Pardon?'

'Whoever he is. Just dump him. You clearly don't have eyes only for him—which suggests to me that you're wasting your time. No woman should be prepared to settle for second-best. And one as pretty as you certainly shouldn't need to.'

She felt her skin burn. How she hated the assumption that she should use her looks to trap a man—though the fact that she was wearing this low-cut sundress meant that she could hardly complain. Oh, dear... Her mother meant so well buying her all these clothes and it would seem so churlish never to wear them...

'I ... There isn't anyone,' she muttered, putting her hand to her throat.

He gave a broad smile and then he laughed. 'In which case let me change my advice, Miss Houndsworth. Don't go ogling men if you aren't prepared to follow it through. Men don't like being treated as sex objects any more than women do. OK?'

'Follow it through?' She almost choked on her words. 'You mean you were expecting me to jump into bed with you? *That's* where I went wrong?'

He shook his head very slowly, looking both surprised and amused at her suggestion. 'Not that. We would only have had seven minutes anyway—but that *wasn't* what I meant.'

'What did you mean?'

But it was too late. The car door had clunked close and the machine was moving.

Olivia got into her car, clapped her hands to her ears and screamed.

CHAPTER TWO

THIS time Livvy drove right up to the cobbled courtyard. And she'd borrowed a huge white sweatshirt from her brother's wardrobe and a pair of his jeans because her own fitted too well, and she'd tied her hair back as severely as it would consent to being tied back. Her only concession to femininity was a choker consisting of three large hand-painted green beads on a leather thong, sitting at the base of her slender neck. And she only wore that because the neck of the sweatshirt had gaped suggestively.

'Oh. It's you again.'

'Yes. I didn't phone because although I called directory enquiries——'

'Shh.' He eyed her irritably, laying one of his fingers across his lips. 'I haven't had breakfast yet. I have a strict rule—no conversation until I've eaten—no matter who the company might be. You can join me for breakfast, but please don't talk.'

'Oh. Right. Look, I'm sorry to call so early on a Sunday morning but——'

'Later!' The word grated out sharply, but this time his finger touched her lips to silence her.

Livvy steppd back, startled, then looked down at her trainers and frowned. Then she nodded meekly and followed him submissively into the house. He hadn't shaved yet—though as it was still only eight-thirty she couldn't complain at that. He led her through the passages again, back to the modern white kitchen. This time she made a point of watching her feet, determined not to ogle him

23

again, but it wasn't easy. He was wearing a loose cotton shirt in very bold navy and white stripes today, with the tail hanging out over the seat of his blue jeans. It should have improved matters, but it didn't because the curve of his buttocks and the broad planes of his shoulders touched against the expanse of cloth as he moved, hinting very enticingly at the powerful body beneath.

On the white table stood a small hamper. While Livvy shifted her weight from one foot to the other, her chin tucked in but her eyes disobediently looking upwards, he placed a pint of milk, some pieces of fruit and a packet of crisp rolls in the hamper. Then he picked up a Thermos flask and took it over to the kettle. When he made the coffee this time he still didn't use a spoon to measure out the granules.

The white phone on the kitchen wall began to warble. Leon didn't look at it, but he turned his eyes commandingly towards Livvy and nodded. She walked over to the phone and put the receiver to her ear. 'Mr Roche's residence,' she mumbled self-consciously, afraid she might laugh.

'Oh, lord...' sighed an attractive and decidedly feminine voice. 'Don't tell me he hasn't had breakfast yet?'

'Er...no. He hasn't. Can I take a message?'

'Yes,' returned the voice decisively, adding in a bar-racking tone, 'Tell him to get up earlier in the morning. Say Katya says so.' And the conversation finished with a sharp click.

Livvy reached into the pocket of her baggy jeans and extracted the notebook and pencil she had placed there earlier, scribbled the message down, and slid it across the table. He didn't look at it.

At last he seemed satisfied with the breakfast he had prepared and he closed the basket, fastening the buckles deftly with his strong fingers. Without looking at Livvy, or making the slightest gesture to indicate that he was conscious of her presence, he pushed open a door and led the way into the garden at the back of the house. Livvy followed him once more.

They seemed to walk for ages. There was an ornamental lake which Livvy remembered well, and which she would have thought the perfect spot, but in fact he led her well beyond that, through grounds which were increasingly unkempt the further they travelled from the house, and into a field bordered by a narrow stream. Finally he set the basket down on the grass, crouched beside it and unpacked the contents, producing a neatly folded groundsheet from the bottom and spreading it out. Livvy, who had found it impossible to keep up with his excessively long strides, covered the last few yards nervously. What should she do when she got there? Was she expected to sit on the groundsheet with him, or should she stand?

He solved the problem by sitting down and then gesturing her to come and sit beside him. Edgily she approached, and lowered her bottom, taking great care to keep as many inches between them as possible.

The silence was broken by his strong white teeth crunching into a crisp apple, which he continued to hold between his teeth while he poured coffee into both of the plastic flask cups. He handed one to her, moving his arm out sideways in her direction with astonishing precision, given that his eyes were resting lazily on the shiny green surface of the stream. She took it from him rather clumsily, her gaze drawn to the bones of his wrist and the dark hairs which shadowed his forearm rather than the cup itself. Her heart began to pound. Mutely she sipped.

He seemed to go on drinking and eating forever. The muscles of his face moved strongly as he bit and chewed, visible beneath the dense stubble which coated his face from a point beneath his cheekbones, sweeping under the angle of his jaw and halfway down his neck. She balanced her empty cup on the grass beside her and then tentatively stretched out her legs and lay back, screwing her eyes very tightly closed and folding her arms stiffly across her breasts.

The crunching stopped. Was it OK to speak now? She opened one eye a crack. To her amazement she found that he wasn't just looking at her, he was looking at her very closely. His head was hovering over hers, his glossy black curls crisply outlined against the clear blue sky, and, what was more, his head was coming nearer.

The sensation which hit her when his mouth finally landed on hers was electrifying. The tart flavour of apples was fresh on his lips, but it wasn't that which produced the shudder which ran through her. It was the taste of the man himself, unmistakably male and even more unmistakably sexual. His firm lips, whose curves she had been able to visualise perfectly even with her eyes tight closed, probed against her own generous mouth. The tip of his tongue was hard and moist and compelling as it ventured against her lips, seeking the interior. Mesmerised by the force of the sensations rippling through her, she allowed it in.

His fingers seemed to have found their way into her hair, too, and were tenderly massaging her scalp, loosening the wayward strands as they rhythmically stroked back and forth. His barbed chin ground against her own smooth skin as the kiss gathered momentum, his tongue probing beyond her teeth as, to her chagrin, she found her own tongue mirroring his movements.

And that was all the contact there was. Their mouths moved in unison and his fingers stroked her head and their faces jostled one against the other. None the less, her breasts, crushed beneath her folded arms, throbbed with excitement, and deep inside her a pulse thundered in response. She was stunned by the power of her own response—too shocked to reject his mouth as long as it drew from her these astonishingly potent sensations. So it was just as well that he elected to stop when he did.

He drew his head slowly away from hers, freed his hands and knelt up straight, looking down cynically on her flushed, startled face. The breath she drew in—which was meant to steady her—caught in her throat and made her jump.

'Well, thank you,' he said slowly. 'That was very nice.'

Livvy's mossy-green eyes opened very wide. 'Uh...' A vacuum seemed to be occupying the space where her brain used to be. What should she say?

'I'm sorry that I didn't ring to warn you that I'd be coming but I couldn't trace your phone number,' she said primly at last, her limbs rigid and her heart beginning to drum madly. 'I know you must think that I have an awful cheek just turning up here again, especially so early on a Sunday, but I was afraid that if I left it any later in the day I might miss you.' Damn it. Her voice was *shaking*! She clamped her bruised lips together firmly and breathed in through her nose.

His blue eyes flashed even bluer, and one of his small smiles began to glow—very slowly, like a smouldering ember in a gentle breeze. 'So you didn't want to *miss* me, eh, Miss Houndsworth? How touching to think that you might have spent yesterday missing me... So that's why you came back?'

Livvy unfolded her arms and scrambled into a sitting position, her face burning. 'Now look, that wasn't what I said. I said that I didn't want to *miss* you. It's quite different, though I'm sure you knew perfectly well what

I meant, anyway. And...um...' She gulped and threw him a stricken look. 'Oh, dear. I'm sorry if I sounded rude just then. Thank you for the kiss. It was certainly very nice, but it wasn't what I came here for. Not at all.'

He tilted back on his heels and watched her coolly as she fumbled frantically for the right string of words.

'I'm sorry about yesterday, too. I suppose I wasn't very...well, whatever it was I should have been. Friendly. Pleasant. Whatever... And the thing is, I really didn't mean to upset you or offend you at all, because why would I? I don't know anything about you, for a start. But the thing is, Mr Roche——'

'Leon. I think it had better be Leon in the circumstances, don't you?'

'Oh. Yes. Yes, of course. Leon. Um... Anyway, the thing is...' She tailed off mournfully. 'I've forgotten what I was going to say,' she confessed at last.

'Shall I prompt you, Olivia? You were saying "the thing is".'

Livvy frowned worriedly. 'You called me Miss Houndsworth a moment ago.'

'Yes. But since we've established that we both thought the kiss was—"nice"?—I imagined that I could assume we were on first-name terms.'

'Oh. Right. Yes. But the thing is, although the kiss was...nice...I don't want you to get the wrong idea. I mean, I didn't come here for that, whatever impression I might have given yesterday, and I don't really think we should do it again.'

He blinked once to acknowledge that he had heard her, but he didn't reply.

Livvy swallowed then continued more firmly, 'The thing is, I was worried by what you said about having the house cleared. You see, I'm not sure if I explained myself very well yesterday, so I just had to come back to stress to you that the document I mentioned is about as crucial to my career as any document could be.'

'You mentioned something of the sort.'

'But I couldn't have got my point across properly...'

'What makes you think that?'

'Because you didn't agree to let me look.'

'Am I obliged to fall in with your plans?'

'No. No, of course not. But the thing is, I'm absolutely desperate that you should, even though you're not obliged to.'

'To the extent of letting me kiss you?'

Livvy's hands flew to her face, then pushed upwards into her hair, loosening it even further. 'No! No, honestly... I'm not like that! That wasn't why I let you do it.'

'You seem prepared to let me do exactly as I please, today, Olivia.'

'Well, that's certainly true—but it isn't why I didn't stop you kissing me although I did come here with the intention of trying very hard not to say or do anything to annoy you.'

'So you've been wanting to say things to annoy me?'

'No. I haven't. I promise.'

'Liar.'

Her cheeks were positively scalding by now. 'Oh, well,' she sighed forlornly, 'only a bit. But what am I supposed to do? If I let you goad me into saying critical things I may as well tear up my work and throw it to the four winds because I'll never get it finished without your co-operation. So what else am I to do but agree with you? You're being very unfair, trying to make me admit that I don't really want to agree with you, because I've never wanted to be more agreeable in my entire life.'

There was a silence, and then his eyes shone from beneath his lowered lids and his mouth broke into one of its unexpected smiles. 'I can believe that,' he said wryly. 'So why did you let me kiss you?'

'Well...' She bit down on her lip and sighed furiously. 'That's an impossible one to answer too, isn't it? Because I won't be able to say right for saying wrong, will I?' Her brow furrowed. 'Yesterday you sort of accused me of...hrrmph——' she cleared her throat '—well...asking for it and then not giving out what I'd supposedly asked for. So if I say I let you kiss me because I...' she screwed her fists into knots and grimaced '...because I *wanted* you to, then you'll think you were right about what I wanted yesterday, and I'll be put firmly in the wrong. But if I say I didn't want you to do it, then it'll look as if I let you do it in order to get you to allow me to look through the library. And then... Good grief! I certainly don't trade favours like that, and I'm sure that even *you* couldn't think well of me if you thought that I had.' She closed her eyes and breathed out.

'So...?'

'So if you want the truth,' she muttered finally between clenched teeth, 'I didn't want you to do it until you started doing it and then I did. You can make of that exactly what you will. It just happens to be the truth and that's that.'

'But you don't want me to do it again?'

'No.'

'Good. Because I don't want to do it again either. Perhaps now that we've sorted that one out you can tell me exactly what it was you drove fifty miles at breakfast-time to tell me.'

'I...'

He laughed then, that low, rich, omniscient laugh which made her skin prickle. 'You look very shocked,' he said. 'Aren't you used to men telling you that they don't want to kiss you, Olivia?'

Livvy examined the palms of her hands. Then the backs of her hands. Then she pushed the cuticles back on two of the fingers of her left hand. Then she said, 'I've been a freelance illustrator for three years now, and I've been very fortunate so far. Early on I was lucky enough to get a good agent who arranged for me to illustrate a gardening column in a glossy magazine—which is my bread and butter—and he also fixed me up with a publisher who was prepared to give me a chance to do the sort of work which I really want to do, which is writing and illustrating stories. I've done a *Cinderella*—with text on one page and a very high-quality illustration on the facing page—and an Aesop's *Fables* in the same style.'

She looked at him looking impassively at her, and then scowled at the stream. 'Anyway, my luck, I'm sorry to say, seems to be on the turn. The magazine wants to produce its own gardening book, which will mean two years of intensive work for me. And my publishers have given me six months to complete the third and final book on my contract, and they've made it plain it had better be good or there won't be any more. I've got another month before I have to commit myself firmly to the gardening book, but if I've not managed to convince the publishers by then that my story book is going to be good enough to be worth marketing aggressively I shall have to do the gardening one. I can't run the risk of leaving myself without any money.' She sighed, looking pleadingly at him.

He regarded her steadily, his mouth relaxed, but his face still entirely unresponsive.

'I've done all the rough sketches and a good deal of preliminary work on the illustrations and I've begun work on the text,' she continued steadily. 'But I was fourteen when I read the document. I thought I'd remember every single word of it all my life because it's the most beautiful and truthful and meaningful love story I've ever heard, but in fact, now that I'm down to the fine detail, I can't be certain. And I must get it absolutely right—because the story is so important.'

She stopped and looked directly at him. 'This means an awful lot to me, Mr Roche. If I mess this up I won't get another publisher to look at me for a long, long time. And if I do the gardening book I won't have any time for my story books. I feel that this is my last chance. Please can I spend the day searching? I promise I won't steal the story, or transgress any legal boundaries. I've written to Major Fox now, and I'll engage a solicitor first thing tomorrow to make absolutely sure that I'm not doing anything I shouldn't. So please? May I?'

His eyes narrowed fractionally, making him look far more like the astute man in the suit she had seen the previous morning than the sinewy woodcutter who had imprinted himself so firmly on her mind's eye—not to mention her lips. 'Why are your publishers being difficult?'

Livvy chewed at the corner of her mouth before replying. 'I've got copies of my books and all my current work in the car. Perhaps if you'd just like to look at them ... ?'

'Just tell me why you think your publishers are being difficult.'

'Well, the *Fables* came out three weeks after the launch of an American TV cartoon series based on Aesop. There were picture books and comics and all sorts of spin-offs from the cartoon flooding the shops. It killed my book stone-dead. Quite frankly, it just didn't sell.'

'And the *Cinderella*?'

'Didn't sell either,' she admitted bleakly.

'Why not? Don't tell me that it was overshadowed by the unforeseen launch of a Disney film only thirty years previously?'

'Er...no.'

'Was it no good?'

'Um...the illustrations were great. Everybody said they were. I mean, I had reviews in national papers saying that they were wonderful.'

'So where did you go wrong with the text? Did you forget to include the ugly stepsisters?'

'Um...' She lowered her eyes and examined her hands again. 'In a word...yes.'

His face remained immutable, but he was silent for rather longer than usual. 'Wasn't that rather careless?'

'I tried to tell the story from a different angle,' she burst out defensively. 'You see, with all the divorce there is today, lots of children have stepsisters, and I thought that it was a bit unfair to portray them in such an unpleasant light.'

One eyebrow quirked drily. 'So you produced a politically correct version of the story?'

'Uh...yes. I suppose that's one way of putting it.'

'Did it never strike you that the story—which has, after all, stood the test of time—might embody some deeper truths? Like the fact that kids often resent stepbrothers and sisters, and might relish having a story which helped discharge some of their hatred.'

She looked at him dumbly. 'Couldn't you just take a quick look? I can run back to the car and be back here in ten minutes. I've learned my lesson over that one. Honestly.'

But he shook his head, beginning to pack everything into the hamper.

With a weary sigh Livvy got to her feet and stepped off the groundsheet. 'Failed again,' she muttered under her breath.

'You're bound to if that's the attitude you take,' he muttered equally softly.

She turned to face him, despair written into her huge, viridian eyes. 'What did I do wrong this time?' she asked weakly. 'I thought I'd covered every angle.'

He stretched out his hand and very, very softly touched her full lower lip with the dry pad of one finger. 'You let me kiss you,' he said condemningly, his eyebrows gathering above his straight nose in a forbidding frown.

'But...Mr Roche...Leon, that's not fair. I didn't seem to have any choice.'

'Because you're sexually attracted to me?'

'I... Well, I suppose I am. But only in a sort of instinctive way.'

'There's another way?'

'Oh, don't tie me in knots again,' she sighed, putting her hands in her hair and shaking her head. 'I haven't got the heart for it.' And to her horror her eyes started to fill with tears and her lower lip, so recently pliant beneath the touch of his fingertip, curled upwards rigidly in an attempt to prevent her from laying herself bare.

She stuffed her hands in the pockets of her brother's jeans and began marching back across the field as fast as she could.

By the time she got back to her car she was ready to burst into tears. She slumped into the driver's seat, her arms folded and her face as closed and bitter as that of a sulky child. She glanced sideways at her work, piled carefully on the passenger seat, and unfolded her arms to flick contemptuously at it with her fingers. And then her face fell and she groaned. That was what he thought of her work—without ever having seen it! Whereas she had faith in herself... Didn't she? She sat for a while longer, thinking. And then she dragged her shoulder-bag out from between the two seats and extracted the small pouch containing her make-up. Right. The polite approach hadn't worked. She'd just have to try again.

By the time she rang the doorbell for the third time in two days she was already beginning to lose her nerve. By the time the hinges yowled she had definitely lost it. By the time the most daunting male face she had ever seen in her life creased with unashamed laughter, she was ready to run away.

'What is it?'

'Blue eye-pencil. If I got it wrong last time because I let you kiss me, I figured this was the best way to make it quite plain that I had no such expectations this time.'

'You look dreadful.'

'That's the intention. Blue lips are not generally considered kissable. Now can we stop talking about my mouth and get on with looking through my work?'

He simply turned on his heel and began walking across the hall, his shoulders slightly hunched and his hands in his pockets. Her blue lips parted in a grimace as she found her eyes relishing his back view yet again. Oh, well, at least he hadn't closed the door in her face. She scurried after him as fast as she could.

Tantalisingly he led the way into the library.

'Is the intention to mock me? I mean, letting me come in here but not letting me open any of these glass-fronted bookcases?'

He swung around and pulled a wry face. 'Could you go and find a water closet and wipe that dreadful stuff off your face before we begin?'

'A *water closet*?'

'This damned house is full of them—but not for much longer, thank goodness. They'll be ripped out just as soon as I start pulling the place to pieces. There are no less than *eleven* water closets to be junked, believe it or not. I can only assume that one of the major's ancestors had trouble with his kidneys. At any rate, they're so old-fashioned they defy description by any other name. Open any door. You'll soon find one.'

Livvy set her work on the enormous oak table and marched off to find a water closet. Huh! Old-fashioned! Part of this house was Elizabethan! What did he expect? He should get together with her parents... They'd have a lot in common. And then, as she found a dank, austere loo with a small spotted mirror redolent of railway waiting-rooms, she castigated herself bitterly. Her parents, when all was said and done, were generous and kind, whereas Leon Roche was verging on the sadistic. The man was a barabarian.

When she got back both of her published books were wide open, as was the scrapbook of her garden columns. He was turning over the sketches she had prepared for the new book at the speed of light.

She hurried across to stand beside him, determinedly ignoring the lurch of her stomach as she came close enough to inhale his aura.

'Er... if you could just slow down...'

'What for? I've nearly finished.'

'Yes. But you're not looking at them properly.'

'I'm looking at them a good deal more carefully than the average browser in a bookshop would,' he said dismissively, turning the last sketch face downwards. He picked up the draft of the text and scanned it.

Then he walked away from her and sat in a mammoth carved oak chair and folded his arms, his blue eyes surveying her assessingly.

'The illustrations in the books are stunning. Very rich. Very detailed. Mature. Not really kid's stuff.'

'That's why I so much want to use the major's story. It's a sort of fairy-tale for adults. I intend this to be an adult book.'

His mouth hardened. 'A new market?'

'Sort of. There have been one or two things in that line in recent years.'

He gave her a brief nod. 'But not many. You're right. It would need to be marketed very aggressively.'

'Yes,' she agreed hopefully.

He paused, his eyes narrowing, his head tilting slightly to one side, the edge of his thumb running back and forth across the curve of his lower lip. 'Why did you draw the heroine wearing a pair of Doc Marten boots when she was otherwise dressed in eighteenth-century garb?'

Livvy wrinkled her nose. 'Um... it's only one sketch. Actually, I've dropped the idea. In the actual thing I'm going to use a donkey instead. She can lean on it.'

'But why was she wearing them in the first place?'

'I did it to emphasise the fact that she'd become rich and didn't have to rely on her crutch any more. They were meant to be like... um... surgical boots.'

'Did the rich have surgical boots in the eighteenth century?'

'Oh, really!' she exclaimed exasperatedly. 'That's just one *tiny* detail which I'm not even including!'

He made a dismissive movement with one shoulder. 'It may have sounded flippant, but it was a serious question. The point I'm trying to make is that you need to do a great deal of research.'

'I know. That's why I know I can't do this and the gardening book as well!'

There was a silence, during which he continued to peruse her while she stood by the table, glancing back and forth uncertainly between her work and his face.

'No,' he said decisively at last. And then he gave her one of his broad smiles like some horrible parting gift, and added, 'Your gardening illustrations are stunning. Very slick, and with a classy feel to them. Technically they're flawless—and imaginative, too. I should imagine magazines are exceptionally well placed to market their own books. Make sure your agent negotiates a good royalty for you.'

Was that 'no' as final as it had sounded? She couldn't believe it. 'What gives you the right to make pronouncements like that?' she said, her voice not entirely steady. 'Are you in publishing or something?'

'I'm in business. The principles never vary.'

'Yes, but what sort of business? I'll bet it's nothing to do with books or illustrating, is it?'

'I own a large construction firm.'

'Well! How *can* the principles be the same?'

'They are. Invest for the future, Olivia. Get yourself a good deal on the gardening book and five years from now you could be rich enough to squander as much time as you like on fairy-tales for adults.'

'I can't wait five years!' she breathed, her disappointment now so manifest that there was no hope of concealing it. 'I'm young. When I get to your age five years might not seem like a long time, but right now it seems like an eternity.' She gathered up her work and was just about to leave when she turned her flushed face on him and asked bitterly, 'May I at least have the pleasure of knowing where I went wrong *this* time, Mr Roche?'

'I thought we were on first-name terms?' he drawled sardonically.

'Oh, damn you! First-name terms? The first name that springs to mind when I look at you is Rat!'

He shrugged. 'I was a wolf yesterday. I think that may be an improvement.'

'Really? Try *Snake in the grass*, then.'

'Snake...?' he echoed. His mouth opened slightly and his eyes, dark with irony, rested very lazily on her high, flushed cheekbones. ' "The serpent tempted me..." ' he murmured.

'Well, you certainly don't tempt me! And as I'm not going to get an answer to my question I shall take this opportunity of wishing you a very un-fond——'

'The answer is that the story is utter...' He hesitated. 'How do you feel about four-letter words, Olivia?'

'There are a few I could apply to you with great pleasure.'

'Well, there are two in particular which sprang to mind when I read that story of yours. It's... No. I won't use them when trash is a perfectly adequate word. The story is trash, Olivia. That's why I'm turning you down.'

The sun was nauseatingly bright when she got back to her car and jammed the key into the ignition. So why did it never rain when you wanted it to? Just to rub her nose in it, the sun continued to shine all the way back to Bristol.

CHAPTER THREE

LIVVY tried very hard for all of twenty-four hours to resign herself to doing without the manuscript. She was already resigned to doing without her London flat and her London friends and her London freedom in her attempt to get the book finished. And she was almost resigned to doing without time to call her own. She loved her parents and she didn't really mind helping them in the shop. After all, they gave so much to others . . . Well, they gave so much to *her*—it was just a shame so much of it was low-cut and came in such inappropriate colours. So if she could resign herself to all of that, then surely she could make do without the manuscript somehow? She racked her brains trying to think of some good reason why it was a good thing that matters had turned out as they had.

But twenty-four hours turned out to be her limit. After that she resigned herself to concluding that there was nothing good about it at all. She was too young to settle for second-best. And to be forced into it by a snake like Leon Roche! The man was a philistine. He wasn't just wrecking her life—he was wrecking the major's beautiful old house, too. How could the major have ever let him buy the place? He was a thug—a thug whom nobody ever challenged because of his astonishing good looks. Well, it was about time somebody told him a few home truths!

What a stroke of luck that she was going to be in London the following day to sort out a dripping tap for her new tenants! She'd checked. She knew where the head office of his construction company was now, and what was more she knew when he'd be there for an important meeting. She was also quite certain that she no longer had anything to gain by being agreeable.

She swept past his receptionist in the lobby of his modern office block, and then swept past his secretary, whose stricken look informed her that she was heading for the right door.

'Leon Roche. The man himself,' she jeered as she stepped into the room, and then took a jarringly deep breath as she registered the presence of the man himself. He was clad in a black suit with a fine stripe, and a crisp white shirt which accentuated the golden hue of his skin and the darkness of his curls. He was balancing one haunch on the corner of a large, polished table, upon which stood a model of a hideous, over-tall skyscraper; and he had the rapt attention of four or five older men in grey suits.

Eight or ten very ordinary eyes turned to take in her straight-backed form, her auburn hair tossed carelessly over her shoulders, her slender figure enhanced by a businesslike tailored black jacket and straight skirt worn with a cream silk blouse. Two extraordinarily piercing blue eyes slowly raised themselves to scrutinise her very deliberately. Naturally, he didn't speak.

'Mr Roche, I have a few things I would like to say to you.'

He smiled very broadly then, his eyes crinkling at the corners, and said silkily, 'Olivia! You're late. I've been expecting you for at least fifteen minutes now... No matter. It's a delight to see you.'

'Don't do this to me!' she returned warningly. 'Of *course* you weren't expecting me. You're just trying to save face in front of your...colleagues. Aren't you?'

He shook his head dismissively. 'No. I rang your home. Your parents told me that you were in London, and as you'd already called my secretary to ask whether I'd be here, and what time you could expect to find me in the building, I had no reason not to expect you. Incidentally, why didn't you tell me that you're usually called Livvy? If I'd known you preferred it I would have used the name all along. It's sweet.'

She would *not* ask where he'd got her parents' phone number from. Nor comment on his use of the familiar form of her name. If she once allowed herself to be sidetracked by him he would automatically have the upper hand...

'My arrival you *may* have anticipated,' she conceded frostily, 'but you don't know yet why I'm here...'

'No?' He tilted his head to one side, and then said more briskly, 'Do let me introduce you to——'

'Introduce me? Don't bother,' she snapped. 'I should hate to strain your precious vocal cords—especially as I have no way of knowing whether you've breakfasted. Anyway, it's only *you* that I want to speak to—though I have to admit that the prospect of an audience is a wonderful bonus.'

His eyebrows arched with amusement. 'Well, go right ahead... What was it you wanted to say?'

She took a deep breath. 'You're a philistine, Leon Roche,' she declaimed, relishing the feel of the words on her tongue. 'A philistine and a vandal. And on top of that you're the most opinionated, self-satisifed, arrogant, immoral, cynical, unscrupulous, materialistic, sadistic *fink* I have ever had the misfortune to meet.'

He sighed. 'Is that it? I think, on balance, I preferred being likened to a snake in the grass.'

'Snake, jackal, vermin, louse—it's all the same to me. Gentlemen, do you know what this man is planning to do?'

'Come on, guys,' urged Leon drily. 'Guess!'

'Oh, do shut up!' she exclaimed with unalloyed brio. '*I'm* the one who's doing the talking this time! And this time I'm going to say *exactly* what I think, just as you did with me on Sunday. You gave my work no more than a cursory glance, Mr Roche, and then you said exactly what *you* thought—barring obscenities, that is. "Trash" was the word you finally came up with, but I can't help feeling that the word was misapplied. You have a lot to learn about definitions.'

She blinked haughtily. 'I feel that it's about time you understood the *real* meaning of the word trash, Mr Roche. It's what you do best, after all, isn't it? You trash buildings, for a start. Beautiful old buildings which have stood unmolested for centuries. You trash footpaths and trees and wonderful old collections of books and even the air that you breathe—when you use it for speaking, at any rate. But worst of all, Mr Roche, you trash *people*. People like me.' She jabbed a finger censoriously in his direction. 'But this time you've chosen the wrong victim—because I ain't about to be trashed by nobody, least of all by somebody as self-satisfied as you.'

The curve of his mouth settled into an indulgent smile. His eyes narrowed with unmistakable delight. 'Livvy, you're brilliant. Gentlemen, I'd like to introduce you to my future wife, Olivia Houndsworth.'

Livvy's mouth fell wide open, her eyes as round as saucers—before she realised that she was reacting exactly as he wanted.

'Don't listen to him,' she cried above the babble of congratulations. 'It's a lie! An outright fabrication. And what's more it's yet another example of what I was just saying about him. Because the thing is, by making out that we're lovers and that I'm just a woman spurned, he's trying to rob my accusations of any legitimacy—to *trash* me, in other words, gentlemen. Because it's none of it true! We're not lovers and never have been and he has no intention whatsoever of marrying me. Don't you see that he merely said it to diminish me in your eyes?'

'No, I didn't,' said Leon drily, standing up and coming around to her side. 'I said it because it happens to be very much the truth—as my colleagues will discover shortly when they get their invitations to the wedding. Have you brought your diary, Livvy? You can fix it up with my secretary now, if you like. Wednesday or Thursday next week would probably be best.'

Her face crumpled with rage. 'You're doing it again,' she accused.

'Am I? Then let me do it in style,' he said evenly. And with that his arms came around her, filling her brim-full with an extra dose of rage, and swept her up in a fireman's lift. Then he calmly hefted her furiously protesting body through his secretary's office, out into the corridor, and dumped her in a...water closet!

'The executive loo,' he smiled, waving the key. 'Have fun. I'll be back to sort out the details of our wedding later.'

And with that he stepped outside, pulling the door closed so firmly with one hand that her entire massed strength applied to the inside door-handle had no effect whatsoever. The lock clicked tormentingly into place.

He left her there for almost an hour. It gave her plenty of time to work out where she'd gone wrong this time.

At last his beautiful, treacherous face appeared around the edge of the door, looking its usual impassive self.

'Shut up and go away.'

'I haven't said anything yet.'

'You don't need to. You've already said enough. And before we go any further, let me concede defeat. Unequivocally I'm no match for you. I should never have bothered ringing your bell that first time. If I'd had the gift of second sight and a draught of poison about my person I can assure you I wouldn't have bothered.'

'Which one of us would have got the poison?'

'Me, of course. Not much point in wasting it on you... It wouldn't have had any effect, anyway. You're unstoppable, Leon Roche. You probably inject poison intravenously just to keep your tongue in working order.'

'But I thought you enjoyed our kiss?' He made a taunting *moue* in her direction which almost had her screaming.

'Oh, for goodness' sake! I meant that you say such venomous things... That's what I meant,' she screeched hoarsely. Then she stopped herself, uncomfortably aware that he was simply stringing her along and she was allowing herself to be led.

'Venomous things? Like "no", I suppose? Aren't you used to men saying no to you, Livvy? Is that what's made you so angry?'

Livvy closed her eyes and sucked her lips inwards and counted to ten. Then she opened her eyes very wide and said, 'Can we get out of this toilet, please?'

'By all means.' And the door was held wide while she marched out into the corridor beyond.

She stalked off, not having any idea whether she was walking in the right direction, and caring less.

He sauntered beside her. 'I've booked a balcony table at the Street Café. Have you been there yet?'

She stared right ahead. 'No.'

He touched her elbow. 'This way for the lift.'

Furiously she turned the corner.

'You'll enjoy it. The food's excellent.'

'Don't patronise me, Leon Roche. Don't talk to me as if I know nothing at all about restaurants. Naturally I've heard of the Street Café. I'm not ignorant. I know all about the famous new eating place for the filthy rich, but fortunately I've never been so desperate to be fashionable that I've been tempted to try it.'

'Do I take it that you hate the place even though you've never been there?'

'Yes, I do. Just reading about it has been enough to turn my stomach. I mean, it was billed as something special before it ever opened its doors or served a single meal. Well, that's just hype, isn't it? It's pretentious rubbish.'

'It's marketing. That's all. The important thing about the Café is that once it did open its doors and started serving meals it lived up to its promises.'

'Huh. My friends and I *loathe* places like the Street Café. We're dumbfounded that anyone can believe that the magical atmosphere of a really good restaurant can be bought from a team of interior designers and pasted to the walls like wallpaper. And we *abhor* the way that historic docklands buildings are being turned into a play-park for yuppies.'

'You preferred them derelict and crumbling?'

'I . . .' She caught her breath. 'They had a certain integrity then,' she sneered. 'Yes.'

'Well, hopefully you'll be able to stomach sitting at a balcony table with your eyes shut long enough for me to grab a meal and propose to you. I'm extremely hungry.'

Livvy swallowed. She didn't like to be reminded of this man's appetites; not in any form. 'I'm not coming.'

But he took her wrist very delicately between his fingers and just lifted it a little and held it. Livvy squirmed, dragging it away. 'Why did you do that?' she burst out, infuriated by her stupid body for burning so flagrantly at his touch. 'Were you planning to do another of your bone-crunching jobs on it—the way you did when we shook hands? I'm an illustrator. My hands are important.'

He sighed slowly. 'And I'm sufficiently uncouth to mangle your precious hands just because you don't want to eat with me, I suppose? You can be almost unbearably offensive when you put your mind to it, Livvy. Thank God we shan't be married forever.'

They had arrived at the lift door, and Leon had reached out to press the button. She watched his beautiful brown hand do the deed, one long finger straight, the soft, dry pad against the button, while the other fingers curled delectably against his palm. They were not, she had to admit, destructive hands. In fact, they looked alarmingly creative. Jaundiced, she looked away.

'If I'm rude it's because it's the only weapon I have against you,' she muttered fiercely. 'You have the knack of making me feel utterly useless, whatever I do or say. I wish I hadn't come here now. I actually *feel* like trash, believe it or not.' She shook her head dispiritedly.

'Oh, come on...' His voice cajoled, as viscous as treacle, and his hand extended towards her, beckoning her into the lift. 'Far from being useless, you are about to prove yourself extremely useful by marrying me. You'll feel much better about yourself once you've agreed.'

'Why do you keep saying that? Why on earth should you want to marry me, anyway?'

'Well, not because I fell in love with you at first sight, Livvy, that's for sure,' he replied laconically. 'I was thinking of something more in the line of a business arrangement.'

'Humph!' she snorted, registering the gastric lurch as the lift dropped fast and hating it. 'Luckily I'm not in business myself. I don't apply business principles to my own life.'

'Not yet, you don't. But you will.'

'Oh, no! I stopped letting you call the shots on Sunday. I discovered then that it got me absolutely nowhere. I've no intention of backsliding.'

'Let's look upon today as an aberration, shall we? You'll soon get the hang of doing things my way again. But *not* in a lift. I shall spread the balance sheet of your life before you while I eat, and you'll soon see how much more productive your life can become when you start running it according to my principles.'

'Principles. Huh! You don't know the meaning of the word.'

'Then you'll have to teach me once we're married,' he returned drily.

'No. *Absolutely* no. Unless you want to carry me screaming into London's most fashionable restaurant, that is.'

He gave one of his low chuckles. 'Don't tempt me.'

Livvy stoically watched the final numbers flash by on the lift's control panel, and then shuddered with relief as the doors opened. She stepped out ahead of him.

But he was at her side instantly. 'Shall I give you a sneak preview of the projected dividend?'

'Not interested,' she asserted, her chin high.

'One,' he commenced, ticking the item off on his fingers, 'you get to search for your document. Two, you get six months of near isolation to finish your pretty drawings. Three, you get all your expenses paid, so you won't have to do the gardening book...'

She frowned.

'You can live in my house for six months, Livvy...' he stated crisply. 'And search for as long as you like.'

'Six months?'

'That's how long you need, isn't it?'

'Yes. But I don't understand...'

'Now hop into the cab and I'll explain the rest when we've ordered.'

Guided by the compelling power of his hand merely brushing against her elbow, she found herself slumping weakly into the capacious seat of a London cab.

'"The serpent tempted me..."' he murmured once more. Then he pulled the door closed, and, sitting closer to her than was strictly necessary, he added, '"And I did eat."'

'OK. I'll eat,' she flashed back, panicked by her awareness of him. 'But I won't agree.'

The Street Café was nauseatingly attractive: huge and light and airy and wholesome. And the balcony was the perfect place for a proposal. It overhung the grey London water, a sturdy structure of glass and iron, protecting its occupants from the unpredictable London weather, and yet still providing the magical atmosphere of the outdoor bustle of the great city. Livvy scowled, disgusted to find herself firmly in the wrong yet again.

'I give in,' she muttered. 'I'll eat till I burst. And you may as well order me the same as you're having, because I have no doubt that you'll manage to choose the most appetising things on the entire menu.'

'I'm not a hundred per cent perfect,' he allowed airily, leaning back in his chair and tucking the tips of his fingers into the waistband of his trousers. 'That's why I need you to marry me.'

'Huh! You think *I'll* put up with your faults? Is that it?' she asked sarcastically.

He laughed then, his face breaking open, his blue eyes glittering behind the sweep of his long, dark lashes. 'I may not be perfect, Livvy, but I'm not a fool. I need you to marry me for the sake of my business.'

'Roche and Son?' She muttered. 'Why? Do you want to make it Roche and Son and Grandson? You need someone to provide you with a son and heir, is that it?'

He narrowed his eyes and surveyed her with amusement. 'Good gracious. That had never occurred to me. Are you offering?'

'Pumph!' she managed, furious with herself for having unthinkingly made such a suggestive remark.

His mocking smile broadened. 'Not such a good idea, huh? With your beauty and my brains our child could rule the world. But if the poor child also inherited your knack of getting things wrong and my tendency to—er—trash things, we might end up being responsible for the greatest vandal since Genghis Khan.'

'Second greatest,' she snapped furiously, badly unnerved by his reference to her looks. Why did men always assume that a woman would be flattered to be described as beautiful? 'You've already made it to first place and I've told you once today that I think you're unbeatable. The poor kid wouldn't stand a chance.'

Her comment made no impact. Insulting him was like dropping a stone into a pool of water and making no ripples whatsoever. Even the laws of physics, it seemed, gave way to this man. In fact, the humorous light in his eyes intensified as if he was delighted that she was being so bolshie.

'I'm gratified to know that you think so highly of my abilities,' he confirmed. 'None the less, my father hasn't long retired, and I'm enjoying being the only Roche on the board. I'm quite willing to shelve the problem of my eventual heir for some years yet.'

'So why do you need a wife?' she muttered acidly. 'Are you about to go bankrupt? Do you need to put the family home in your wife's name to save you from total ruin?'

His eyes still betrayed amusement, but his mouth hardened slightly. 'No,' he drawled. 'I'm not about to fold. Far from it. I'm expanding. Unfortunately the managing director of the company I'm interested in is adamant that he'll only sell to a married man.'

Livvy frowned. 'I don't understand. Does his firm specialise in building honeymoon hotels or something?'

'No.'

'And anyhow,' she continued in puzzled disbelief, 'how can he afford to pick and choose? If he needs to sell, won't he be obliged to sell to the highest bidder or something?'

'No. He doesn't have to sell for financial reasons. It's his health; he wants to retire. But he also wants to ensure that his business stays much as it is after he's gone. He believes that a married man will prove more sympathetic to his workforce. The contract he's insisting on means that he'll be staying on the board for six months after the take-over and will be able to veto any changes. Assuming he's satisfied with the way things are going, he'll pull out after that.'

'Leaving you to do exactly as you please,' she concluded coldly.

'Yes.'

'Including asset-stripping,' she intoned scornfully. 'Selling off the buildings. Throwing people out of work. Trashing everything in your path. That sort of thing, I suppose.'

He regarded her mildly. 'What a sharp little brain you have whirring away inside that head of yours, Livvy. You should have followed your parents into the family business. You could be running a chain of hypermarkets by now.'

'So I'm right! That is your plan, isn't it? You want to trick this man into believing you're Mr Nice Guy for six months and then you'll set about carving up his firm and throwing people on the unemployment heap.'

He lifted his eyebrows fractionally, and one corner of his mouth quirked sardonically.

'The thing is,' she hurried on stormily, desperately struggling to free her eyes from his utterly gorgeous face, 'I can't for the life of me understand why he'd be fool enough to believe that a wife would alter you one jot. Your reputation has obviously preceded you if he's making stipulations like that. He must know what you're like. So why is he even considering your offer?'

'He knew my father,' Leon replied evenly.

'Knew...?' Livvy echoed. 'I thought you said your father had retired. Isn't he...um...well or something?'

'Yes. He's well or something. Like the major, he too is still very much alive. But he also has retired abroad, which means that he no longer sees all his old friends.'

'Cleared off to some tax haven, I suppose,' she muttered.

He smiled. 'Don't you approve of tax havens, Livvy?'

'I think people should contribute to the well-being of the countries which educated them and nurtured them and trained them,' she replied archly, 'instead of taking their money and running.'

He regarded her coolly for a while, saying nothing. Then he murmured in a low, gravelly, taunting voice, 'You disapprove of quite a number of things, don't you?'

'No more than the average person. I simply believe in honesty and decency and a few other little things which you might not have heard of.' The deep note of his voice had set the hairs on her neck prickling. She shook her

head, clenching her fists on the white tablecloth.
'Honestly... Fancy going to such lengths to trick some
poor old man into destroying his life's work! I feel really
sorry for him—not to mention all the people this deal
of yours is going to damage. You're a barbarian, Leon
Roche.'

His voice still low and mocking, he said, 'I take it that
you don't believe that marriage will civilise me, in
that case?'

CHAPTER FOUR

'NOT the sort of marriage you're planning, no.'

Leon smiled a very broad and very dazzling smile. 'Ah . . . so it's simply the type of marriage which is at fault? You do think that I could be redeemed, perhaps— if only I had the love of a good woman. Is that it?'

Livvy glowered at him. There he sat, looking as stunning as any man could look, mouthing platitudes about being saved by the love a good woman, and the worst of it was she was *tempted*! A juvenile, animal part of her actually wanted to have a go at taming the savage beast. Huh!

'You're not worth saving,' she burst out. 'And anyway, the thing is, I can't imagine for one moment why you picked on me of all people to be your fake wife. I would have thought I'd be the last person you would have asked. Or are you so arrogant that you haven't yet spotted the fact that I don't approve of you?'

'I had noticed.'

'Then why? Why me?'

He tilted his head to one side and quirked his eyebrows. 'You look the part,' he said.

Furiously she glanced down at her clothes. Oh, damn and blast! Why had she worn this suit? She'd actually gone out of her way to look like someone who'd fit into his world today. It had been part of her master plan for humiliating him. With a toss of her head and a haughty thrusting of her fingers into her mass of shining hair she glared at him and said, 'You're forgetting something. I told you exactly what I thought of you in front of all

54

those suits this morning. The story's bound to go the rounds and nobody will believe in your so-called marriage for five minutes.'

He shrugged. 'I'm quite happy for my colleagues to gossip to their hearts' content. It can only improve the situation. Richard Gallagher—he's the man I'm buying out—will be delighted to know that I have such an honourable and principled woman for a wife. And one who's not afraid to stand up to me in public as well. Everybody was enormously impressed by you, Livvy. You did me quite a favour this morning. I couldn't have engineered it better myself. You're one in a million. Did you know that?'

Livvy opened her mouth like a carp, and then shut it again. 'You're incredible!' she exclaimed at last, unnerved by his silent appraisal.

'I'm flattered,' he returned, dazzling her with his smile.

'Oh, for goodness' sake! Leave me alone. Sort out your own problems.'

'Problem,' he returned emphatically, putting his elbows on the table and leaning towards her. 'I have only one problem, which you are shortly going to solve for me. I have no spouse.'

'I can understand why.'

He looked at her with an air of benign amusement. 'Don't mock. *Your* problem is far worse,' he said. 'You are having to face up to the prospect of spending two years drawing heaps of well-rotted manure from life instead of painting angel-faced heroines bent over their spinning-wheels and lovelorn heroes on horseback, not to mention all those lavish borders of guelder-roses on midnight-blue grounds. I stand to lose a good business opportunity, Olivia,' he concluded hollowly. 'You stand to lose your soul.'

'I can handle it.'

He regarded her sardonically. He was right, of course. She'd let her flat in town and moved back home to finance her work and had given up her friends and her social life and still it wasn't working.

'It's no hardship to live at home,' she muttered.

He went on looking.

Her brother was the worst, playing his heavy metal music on his CD-player well into the small hours. But Ian was a first-year medical student and her parents wouldn't let her complain, saying that he was just a teenager, and he needed to get this stuff out of his system now as he would have years of hard work ahead of him before he became a doctor.

'I don't mind helping in the shop. It's a small price to pay for my board and lodge,' she insisted.

Still he said nothing.

'My parents have worked incredibly hard to make their shop profitable over the years,' she went on defensively. 'I'm delighted to be able to help them.'

'It's not helping you get your work done, though,' observed Leon reasonably.

'It's helping them. They've made a thriving business out of a little corner shop. They deserve a break after all the hard work they've put in.'

'If their shop's profitable, why don't they employ help?'

Livvy sighed and pushed her fingers through her hair. 'Your idea of profit and their idea of profit are worlds apart, Leon,' she explained irritably. 'You come from the world of big business while they live in the world of small businesses. If they employed someone then they wouldn't have that extra bit of cash which they consider a good profit. And anyway, they wouldn't trust an out-sider in their shop. They know their customers—and they care about them. I know them too, so they feel happy leaving me in charge.'

'Surely you can't be the only person they trust? Your brother answered the phone to me.'

'Ah. Well, Ian's a medical student. He has to study.' He shrugged.

'I don't mind helping,' she persisted. 'They live over the shop, Leon. The premises are modest, although Mum and Dad lavish a great deal of loving care on their home. My parents are...' she paused, searching for the right words '...hard-working, practical and generous to a fault. But they are not imaginative people. They don't quite understand what it is that I want from life and why.' Livvy bit down on her lower lip. 'They expect me to be see the world through their eyes, that's all.'

Leon laid one finger across his lips and watched her carefully as she spoke. Then he shrugged slightly. 'That's great. But it's not helping you get your book finished, is it? And your lack of financial independence isn't really helping them come to terms with the things that you want from life either, is it?'

It was true that they'd been very proud of her when she'd established herself so quickly after college and were utterly baffled by the fact that she was giving it all up for a dream.

He slanted a wry look at her. 'Wouldn't they like to see you as mistress of Purten End?' he teased.

'For six months? While you ripped the place to pieces? Big deal.'

He shrugged. 'There'd be the divorce settlement at the end of it, of course.'

'You mean I'd get to keep the house?' she queried incredulously.

He pulled a resigned sort of face. 'I'd have to contest it. But then again, as the joint marital home, it could go either way...' He shrugged again.

Livvy looked away from his honey-gold face, the symmetry of his strong features, the blue-black lustre of his curls and the mesmeric depths of his eyes. Just sitting at the same table with him was worse than any calculated seduction. She bitterly resented the pull his appearance exerted on her. She didn't believe in judging people by their looks, and Leon Roche of all people deserved to be judged entirely by his actions. So why were her eyes and her stomach approving of him so flagrantly?

'I'd never marry for money,' she said contemptuously.

'Excellent. You sound just like the sort of wife Richard Gallagher has in mind for me.'

'Oh, shut up.'

'And if you refuse to pursue your joint interest in the house when the marriage is over it will suit me down to the ground. What could be better than that, Livvy? Everybody gets what they want.'

Livvy chewed on her lower lip. 'You mean the house would be half mine while we were married?' she asked uncertainly.

'Mmm. In principle.'

'So I could stop you modernising it, could I?'

His eyes laughed. 'Now why should you want to do that, Livvy?'

'You're forgetting that I've been in Purten End before. I remember what it used to be like. I've already seen what you've done to the kitchen—and if that's any indication of what you intend doing to the rest of the house, then the sooner somebody stops you from destroying the spirit of it the better. It used to be incredible, that kitchen. It used to have an open hearth with a real spit for roasting meat.'

'Very handy,' he said with a wry smile. 'Just the ticket for heating up a tin of beans.'

'That's not the point!' she burst out. 'It was historic. There was even a dog-wheel for turning the spit.'

'Two lamb chops and a Jack Russell, please,' he returned scathingly, raising his eyebrows. Then he put the tips of his fingers on the edge of the table. 'It's up to you, Livvy.'

She didn't deign to reply. He, in the meantime, yawned widely as if her reply was of no consequence anyway. In doing so he revealed all of his strong, even white teeth. Couldn't the man even have had a single filling some-where along the way? She clamped her lips together and glowered.

'I'm not in the business of forcing you,' he said calmly at length.

She managed not to reply.

He smiled. 'Tempted?' he asked softly.

'No, I am *not* tempted,' she wailed, knotting her hands in her lap.

'Shame on you, to let such a historic old house be decimated! Good lord, Livvy. Just what *are* these prin-ciples which govern your life?'

She pressed her hands to her cheeks and glared at him. 'How do you do it? How do you manage to put me in the wrong at every turn? Surely it's very high-minded of me to refuse to marry you for the sake of your business and my convenience? Marriage ought to be anything *but* a business arrangement, for goodness' sake! And yet I seem to find myself turned into the villain of the piece just because I have faith in love! I can't believe this is happening.'

He tilted back in his chair and smiled at her, regarding her coolly over his high cheekbones. 'OK. Have it your own way. Any female will do, actually, as long as she's single and willing. And in my experience there are plenty of those around.'

Livvy glared at him. 'Is that what you think of women?'

He shook his head carelessly. 'Only the single and willing ones. They do exist, I'm afraid, Livvy, no matter how high-minded and romantic a view you choose to take of the world. At any rate, I don't imagine that it will be difficult to find a substitute. But I have to confess that I'm disappointed in you. I thought that you might be pleased to have all your problems so neatly resolved.'

'All my problems resolved? When I'd be gaining *you*?' she cried incredulously.

'Only occasionally. Only at weekends. And for functions in town now and then.' His brow creased fleetingly. 'Oh, don't worry, I wouldn't expect you to *sleep* with me. You didn't imagine that I meant that you should, did you?'

'No-o...'

He let out a huge bellow of laughter. 'Tempted now, Livvy?'

'No. Certainly not.'

He quirked his eyebrows drily.

'Why should I be tempted by the prospect of *not* sleeping with you?' she asked stiffly.

'Why? Would you like to?'

'No.'

'Well, then. What's the problem?'

The problem was, she found herself thinking, that, much as she didn't want to sleep with him, she didn't want to have to spend six months fighting the temptation to do something she didn't even want to do. 'Nothing. There isn't one.'

'Oh?'

Somewhere along the way their food had arrived. As he spoke that single word he slipped a morsel of scallop between his lips and all the blood seemed to drain from Livvy's face at the sight. She had never found any man attractive in the way that she found Leon attractive. She was becoming aroused just by watching him eat!

'I can't imagine why you should think I'd be over-whelmingly tempted to do anything with you, Leon Roche,' she bit out with asperity, studying her plate and finally stabbing a scallop viciously with her fork.

He breathed in deeply through his nose. 'Aside from all the problems the marriage would solve in your life, there's the question of your being able to put your precious story to the test. Doesn't that idea tempt you? You could prove once and for all that it wasn't trash. You could prove me wrong, Livvy. Don't you see?'

'No. I don't see actually...' She tailed off. The truth was that she did see, actually. She saw only too well.

'Let me point out the parallels,' he said, laying down his fork and chewing. 'Beautiful but poor heroine. Rich hero. Marriage contracted on the understanding that it is no more than an arrangement of convenience, and will not be consummated. Marriage to last for six months.'

'You're missing out all the bits that don't fit,' she replied thornily. 'Like, for instance, the fact that the hero loves the heroine. Like, for instance, the fact that she's crippled and fears that his love will not last when he finds out how burdensome life with her will be. Like, for instance, the fact that the whole point of their getting married but not consummating the marriage is for her to prove to him that he only loves her beautiful face, and will tire of her in the end.'

'That's not why *he* agrees to the marriage.'

'Well, no. He agrees because he believes that she will come to love him during their time together. He hopes she'll stay when the six months are up. Even so, I can't see what any of it has to do with us. You don't love me and I certainly don't love you. And don't try telling me that you'll be begging me to stay on as your wife when the six months are up, because we both know that nothing could be further from the truth.'

'So you aren't tempted even a tiny bit?'

'No! Of course I'm not. Honestly, you are so arrogant! Fancy imagining that I'd marry you just to make you richer.'

'What about all the bits on the balance sheet which accrue to you?'

'No! No woman in her right mind would agree to marriage for any reason other than mutual love.'

'The heroine in your story did.'

There was a horrible and very prolonged silence. Leon ate his steak and salad with apparent hunger. Livvy kept putting bits of food in her mouth and then finding that the more she chewed, the less able she was to swallow. She washed down her meal with wine, frowning at her plate and scarcely daring to let her eyes drift upwards in case they met those of the most beautiful and unscrupulous man she had ever met in her entire life.

'A marriage,' she replied at last, keeping her eyes lowered, 'a true marriage,' she reiterated stiffly, 'isn't a legal contract anyway. It's not made when the vows are taken or when the register is signed. It's made on the wedding night. In the story that didn't happen and was never intended to happen. In fact, until it happens a marriage is null and void even in the eyes of the law.'

'A technicality. It sounds to me as if you're ready to agree with me that your story is trash.'

'The story's not trash,' she muttered bitterly after a very long time, surprised to feel her face burn scarlet as she said it. 'It's a wonderful, honest love story.'

'It's a common-or-garden tale of sexual infatuation. He fancies her, and she can't resist his power and wealth. There's nothing original or particularly beautiful about that.'

'He *loves* her.'

'He can't possibly. He doesn't know her. He proposes to her without ever having spoken to her. She's just a face at the window to him.'

'It was love at first sight.'

Leon shrugged.

'But she rejects his power and wealth.'

'Not for long, she doesn't.'

'She does! She only marries him because she can't bear to see his torment—not because she wants his money.'

'She's an eighteenth-century peasant girl with a duff leg. What in heaven's name is she doing being so noble? It doesn't make sense. I mean, do you have any idea what her life expectancy would have been if she hadn't married him?'

'She didn't plan to *stay* married to him. She intended to return to her old life when the six months were up.'

'But she didn't, though, did she?'

'Well, no! That's the whole point of the story. But she only stayed with him because she truly fell in love with him.'

'Really? Are you sure that she did? Power and wealth are supposed to be powerful aphrodisiacs.'

'Huh. If you confine your attention to women who are single and willing, then I can well imagine why you might be inclined to think that *all* women can be seduced by power and wealth. But you're wrong.'

'So I can take it you would never be corrupted by something so base?'

'Damn right I wouldn't. And nor would Rosamund in the story. The story's about *love*, Leon. Not about lust and avarice.'

'Are you so sure?'

'Yes. Yes, I am. One hundred per cent sure. For goodness' sake, that's why I want to make a book out of the story! I think it's important!'

'So you're planning a sort of counter-blast to all the sex-and-shopping novels that top the bestseller lists?'

'Yes. If you like.'

'You have a mission to do this book, then? To set the world to rights in your own very peculiar way?'

She tossed her head. 'You can mock my ideals as much as you like. I won't budge.'

He raised his eyebrows scornfully. 'You're all hot air, Livvy. You live in a fantasy world. If you lived in my house for six months as my wife, you'd find out a damned sight more about sexual attraction and the pleasures of material wealth than you'll ever discover from fairy-stories.'

She glared at him. 'You hypocrite! You said that if I were to marry you you wouldn't expect me to sleep with you.'

'Of course I wouldn't!' His clear blue eyes lobbed a dart of disgust in her direction. 'Good grief, woman, I wouldn't claim conjugal rights just because we'd stepped into a register office together for a few minutes. What the hell do you take me for, Olivia? However, you've already made it quite plain that you find me attractive, and I myself am not unaware of your physical charms. Put us together in a country house isolated from the rest of the world for goodness knows how long and who knows what might happen? I certainly wouldn't refuse to sleep with you on *principle*.'

'But you said... I mean, on Sunday you said that you didn't want to kiss me again.'

'That's right. You said the same thing.'

'Yes, but I said it because I really didn't want to kiss you again. On principle, actually.'

He sighed impatiently. 'And I said it because I didn't particularly want to kiss someone who was quite clearly going to balk at kissing *me* again. For crying out loud, Livvy, you kept your arms folded! It was quite obvious you weren't going to let yourself enjoy that kiss one iota more than you had to. But when I find a woman attractive in the way that I find you attractive, Livvy, I don't like having to ration myself. I'm not a schoolboy any more. I'm a normal, adult male. I'd much rather do without than kiss someone who's holding back on *principle*.'

Livvy frowned at him, astonished to discover that he'd perceived her to be holding *anything* back when he'd kissed her! Her memory of the event was dominated entirely by the complete lack of restraint which her senses had displayed. She eyed him uncertainly. 'Then presumably if I did move into your house for six months, then...um...nothing at all would happen.'

'Presumably. If you really do have all those principles you claim to have, that is.'

'Clearly *you* don't have any,' she flashed back archly.

'If you mean by that will I be a virgin on our wedding night, Olivia, then the answer has to be no,' he said with a laconic sigh. Then he began to drum his fingers irritably on the table-top. 'Look, Livvy, I just figured that we were both mature enough to handle this without any problems. I figured that you'd get what you wanted and I'd get what I wanted. I also assumed that if, by mutual agreement, some time within that six months we felt like going to bed together then we probably would because we'd be mature enough to handle that too. I obviously got you wrong. Perhaps I should never have suggested this marriage business at all. But as you seemed to find the idea of an unconsummated marriage of convenience perfectly acceptable in this wretched story of yours, I didn't figure it would be a problem for you in real life.'

'You obviously have a very low opinion of me,' she complained crossly.

He raised his shoulders dismissively. He didn't say anything.

'Well?' she demanded.

He took a long draught of water from the crystal tumbler before him. Then he said drily, 'Yes. I think I must do.'

'What is it this time? I mean, where have I gone wrong now?'

'How old are you? Twenty-four? Twenty-five? Old enough to have learned a little more about life than you seem to have managed so far, at any rate. No wonder you want to write fairy-stories for grown-ups. I wonder how many people will want to *read* them, though—if ever you manage to finish this book between helping in the shop and studying dwarfing rootstock, that is.'

'I simply have a few ideals, that's all!' she burst out, burning with indignation.

'Ideals? So you keep saying, but what the hell *are* they? You're supposed to be committed to your own work but you won't take the opportunity to get on with it when it's offered. You're committed to this old story but you won't grab the chance to find the original document and make sure you get it right. You're committed to love, but as far as I can work out you're not actually *in love* with anyone at all. I mean to say, Livvy, what does it all boil down to? You don't honestly believe that a nobleman on a white charger is going to gallop into your parents' shop and demand your hand in marriage along with his pound of apples, do you? And what will you do then, Livvy? How will you proceed? You've got principles. It could never work.'

Impossibly, Livvy began to laugh when he said that. She put her hand over her mouth and shook silently with it, her eyes wide with consternation. She pinched her nose. 'I'm going to stop laughing in a minute,' she promised shakily, and took a gulp of wine. She bit extremely hard on her full lower lip and then said, 'I didn't mean to laugh, you know. It was just such a stupid image. I couldn't help myself.'

His eyelids drooped a little at the corners and he regarded her with an expression that verged on disbelief.

Livvy wriggled her shoulders inside her black jacket and frowned. 'Look. I can't help having ideals. I've always had them. It's the way I am.'

He raised his eyebrows disparagingly and sighed deeply, as if genuinely appalled. 'You can surely help having principles which mean nothing at all? Why don't you just opt for doing without? It would save a lot of time.'

'Yeah . . . and end up like you? No, thanks.'

'Are you sure that what you've got is worth such a lot?' he asked softly.

She picked up her bread roll and broke off a piece jerkily. Then she dropped it on her plate, turning her fierce eyes full on to his face. 'Why are you wasting time arguing with me? Why aren't you off looking for someone who's single and willing? I'm sick of this conversation.'

He leaned back in his chair and watched her for a moment, his lower lip jutting slightly. Then one corner of his mouth tightened. 'I want to get this take-over in the bag as soon as possible. It's a question of timing, Livvy. You're here. Any other potential Mrs Roche is out there somewhere,' and he jerked his head towards the door. 'I don't have time to go looking. It has to be you.'

She buried her face in her hands. She covered her eyes with her fingertips and pressed hard. Well, damn it to hell, she felt sorry for him now. She felt sorry for him because he was so busy and powerful and rich and successful and good-looking. Damn... The people she should feel sorry for were those poor men and women who were going to be thrown out of work in six months' time, for want of a good woman to civilise Leon Roche.

She peered into the colours created by the pressure of her fingers on her eyelids: golden-brown haloed by black, with pin-pricks of electric blue. She dropped her hands, letting them puddle helplessly on the green-striped tablecloth, keeping her eyes firmly closed. She chewed her top lip and then, after a while, she chewed her bottom lip. Then she rubbed the palms of her hands together and opened her eyes.

CHAPTER FIVE

'WELL?'

'Well what?'

'All that face-pulling . . . It looks to me as if the negotiations are complete. Do we have a deal?'

'Nope. Sorry.'

He expelled air through his nose. 'You're just being obtuse now. It's called cutting off your nose to spite your face.'

Livvy shook her head and gave him a bitter smile. 'It's not, actually. It's called moving back home with your folks. My mother and father would never wear it, and I've got far too much respect for them to deceive them.'

He eyed her narrowly, shaking his head very slowly.

'It's *true*,' she added emphatically.

'So that's really your only reservation now? Your parents' reaction? You were that close to agreeing?'

Livvy studied him pensively. 'Yes. I think for a brief moment I probably was.' And with that she buttoned her jacket over the cream silk blouse and smoothed down her skirt preparatory to getting up.

But Leon beat her to it. Briskly scrunching his napkin in his big, bronzed hand, he got to his feet and dropped the crumpled cloth carelessly on to the table. Then he came round behind her to pull out her chair. 'Where did you leave your car?'

'Islington. Outside my flat. Or what used to be my flat, anyway. Why? Are you offering to escort me?'

He glanced at his watch. 'No. I haven't time. But I'll call you a cab.'

'Don't bother,' she said sweetly, twizzling a strand of her rich, auburn hair away from her face. 'I can find my own way in this world without *your* help. I've been doing it for quite some time, believe it or not.' And with that she walked away from him very fast.

She went back over that moment time and again on the drive home to Bristol. It should have felt good. He hadn't tried to catch up with her or throw her over his shoulder or do anything cavemanish like that. Apparently she had persuaded him to take her seriously. But every time she began to gloat her heart would end up sinking. She might have convinced him that she wasn't tempted by him—which, ironically, wasn't strictly true—but it hadn't brought her any nearer to getting her hands on the major's document, had it? And, much worse, she now felt as if she had the livelihoods of goodness knew how many working people on her conscience. Let alone a fine old Elizabethan house somewhere in the Herefordshire countryside.

By the time she was off the motorway and stuck in a rush-hour traffic jam she had stopped gloating altogether. She was appalled by the weight of the load she was carrying. Apparently the only hope for hundreds, maybe thousands of people, let alone the heritage of the English nation, depended entirely on the civilising influence of a good woman. And, to be fair to herself, she'd always tried very hard to be good. That was what her much vaunted principles were all about, wasn't it? Whereas the next single and willing woman Leon stumbled across might be ... well, just anybody.

What was it he'd said? That her principles didn't amount to much? She gulped hard, running her fingers through her hair as she waited for the last set of traffic lights to change. Oh, dear. She'd better try ringing him as soon as she got home. He could bump into a single, willing and unprincipled woman at any moment... And—she screwed up her face in agonised anticipation—she'd force herself to tell her parents the absolute truth about it all. They'd never understand in a million years; they'd think she was crazy; but it couldn't be helped. At least her parents had a secure living and a roof over their head, even if the bathroom was unfashionably green.

Resigned, she pushed open the glass door at the side of the shop and made her way into the luxuriously carpeted passage. Her mother's feet came pattering down the stairs.

'Livvy! Thank goodness you're back. Why didn't you tell us about your friend Mr Roche?'

'Oh, yes.' She sighed wearily. 'He rang this morning, didn't he?'

Her mother caught hold of her by the shoulders and then began to smooth her hair back from her high forehead with her fingers just as she had done when Livvy had been a small girl. 'Quick! Put a bit of lipgloss on. He's upstairs in the sitting-room now.'

She couldn't honestly claim to be surprised, though it was galling to note how speedily he'd managed the journey. No doubt he'd come here to harangue her again. He wasn't the sort of man to give up easily, when all was said and done. Well, she'd save him the effort. Just as soon as she got him on his own she'd tell him that she was ready to give in.

'Mum, why are you smiling?'

'Am I?' Moira Houndsworth tucked her chin in and tried to frown. 'I'm not. Am I?'

'You're smirking actually.'

Her mother arched her faded eyebrows. 'Oh, well. You know... He's that sort of man, isn't he? He knows how to put people at their ease. And anyway, pet, it's all so exciting.' And then she gave Livvy an impulsive and decidedly uncharacteristic hug. 'Any mother would smile, wouldn't she?'

'Mu-uum...' Livvy sighed, opening her eyes very wide and pushing her hands nervously into her jacket pocket. 'The thing is... look, wait a minute. Tell me what he's said.'

But her mother had no intention of waiting. 'Now come along, Livvy. Hurry up. At least you've got that smart suit on that I bought you for Aunty Milly's wedding.'

Livvy's brain buzzed as she padded upstairs towards the first-floor lounge. 'What exactly has he told you?' she muttered over her mother's shoulder.

'Oh. Everything, I think. More or less. Now be quiet or he'll hear you.'

He was sitting to one side of the imitation coal fire which danced prettily in the grate, and was drinking a cup of tea, the saucer set on a veneered table beneath the outstretched arm of a china ballerina. He held the cup between the fingerpads of both hands, almost miraculously seeming to make the delicate piece of porcelain appear to fit with his big frame.

He turned his head directly towards Livvy when she came into the room and gave her one of his very piercing looks. She returned it with what she hoped was a suitably reptilian glare.

'Well, well,' she said haughtily. 'What on earth brings you here, Mr Roche?'

He began one of his slow, simmering smiles. 'Now, Livvy... no need to be coy. I've explained absolutely everything to your parents.'

'Everything?' she echoed, alarm beginning to thunder through her like hoofbeats.

Leon's hooded eyelids flickered an amused assent.

'He's asked for your hand, Livvy,' said her father, choking back emotion, and when Livvy turned to meet his eye she found that he was beaming with manifest joy, his eyes extraordinarily bright. 'I'm that proud. It's very unusual for a man to show so much respect for a father in this day and age.'

Livvy gulped, horrified. She swung her head round to look at her mother who was dabbing at the inner corner of one eye with a pink tissue. And still smirking. 'Fancy falling in love at first sight.' She sighed enviously. 'Of course, we never had the opportunities for doing things like that in our day, did we, Dad?' She turned to Leon and explained confidingly, 'There wasn't the money about like there is nowadays. We had to court for years and years and save every penny then.' She paused. 'People fell in love at first sight in the war, of course, but that was different. There was a war on.'

Leon smiled warmly at her mother and then said, 'Even so, Mrs Houndsworth, as I mentioned earlier, it's going to be a big jolt for Livvy despite the fact that we're so much in love. She's a bit shell-shocked, aren't you, darling? In fact, she told me earlier today that she was worried about how you would take it—didn't you, Liv?—which only goes to prove that her mind's in something of a whirl.'

Livvy's mouth opened and then closed.

'Happy, love?' her father murmured to her.

Puppet-like, she forced her head to nod a grindingly stiff nod. And then forced her dry lips to smile.

'Worried about us?' echoed her mother, frowning. 'Good grief, Livvy, what's the matter with you? He's so...' and she gave what was intended to be a discreet jerk of her head in Leon's direction and waggled her eyebrows suggestively '. . . nice,' she breathed emphatically. 'He's just the sort of man we'd always hoped you'd meet, what with your *looks* and talent for sketching and everything.' Then she turned to Leon and said firmly, 'We're delighted, Mr Roche. We couldn't be more thrilled, could we, Dad? Don't you pay any attention to our Livvy. She has funny ideas at times but they don't amount to much at the end of the day. She's a lovely girl. Her heart's always been in the right place.'

'But the thing is,' began Livvy, her mouth feeling unnaturally rigid, 'er. . . although we've. . . um. . .' she closed her eyes briefly and gulped '. . . fallen in love at first sight——' her voice sounded practically strangulated at that point '—we. . . um. . . well, we hardly know each other. I don't think you should dismiss my. . . um. . . pre-wedding nerves so lightly.'

Leon stood up very slowly then and walked across the room towards her. He fixed his eyes hard upon hers and gave her one of his dazzling smiles. Then he rested his wrists on her shoulder and looked meltingly into her panic-stricken green eyes. 'Sorry, Liv. . .' he murmured ruefully. 'Perhaps I shouldn't have come here without telling you first, huh? But I couldn't wait another minute for you to agree to be my wife.' He paused to pop an insincere kiss on to the tip of her nose. 'And I couldn't bear to think of you worrying your pretty little head unnecessarily about how to tell your parents.' The next kiss landed on her forehead. 'It hurt me, Livvy, darling.' He cradled her right cheek in one broad palm and pressed the other cheek against his faithless heart at that point. The strength in his arms was phenomenal. Even more phenomenal was the fact that a human heart actually appeared to beat within him. She could hear it, loud against her hot cheek, before she inched away.

'It wounded me,' he continued almost plaintively. 'You see, I just knew your parents would be as blissfully happy as we are when they heard the news. All your foolish little doubts...' He sighed heavily. 'Oh, darling, surely you see? You don't need to worry any more. I've come here to resolve that last little lingering problem of yours.' And he tapped the end of her nose with one finger and murmured very softly and very sarcastically, 'Your virtue is still intact.'

Livvy felt her face scorch crimson. While he had been speaking he had drawn her fractionally closer to him so that his jacket brushed against her breasts, sending them into paroxyms of delight. The fingers of one hand had travelled delicately beneath the mantle of her hair and his thumb stroked the nape of her neck.

'Was that very naughty of me?' he cooed in an apologetic, little-boy voice which was so false that she almost laughed. He moved the hand which had tapped her nose back to her shoulder and squeezed it firmly. She felt the soft fingerpads of those oh, so creative hands nudge against her flesh, creating some swimmingly erotic sensations deep within her, and she caught a spark of malicious mirth in the depths of his blue, blue eyes, though his face was all tender concern.

'It was very, very naughty of you,' she muttered testily, and then cleared her throat. Her voice had gone all wobbly and strange.

He gave a low chuckle and drew her closer again, so that now her breasts brushed enticingly against his shirt-front.

'Ahh,' sighed her mother loudly, in the tone of voice reserved for kittens on TV.

Livvy forced her head sideways so that she could see her parents, who were now standing side by side, their arms linked, and beaming sweetly. 'The thing is,' she said, casting them a sickly smile, 'you see, because we don't know each other very well, I'm worried that we'll marry in haste, and...um...you know... I mean, the thing is, Mum and Dad, suppose in a few months, six months, say, we discovered that...um...?'

'We won't,' said Leon determinedly, grasping her chin and pulling her face around to meet his. 'Love conquers all, Livvy. You of all people should know that. It's the theme of your new book, after all, and it's going to be the theme of your new life as well.'

Livvy considered screaming, but didn't trust her voice.

'Well said,' muttered her father gruffly.

'Yes, but the thing is——'

Leon dropped a kiss on her forehead. 'Shh...' he murmured lovingly. 'We're different, aren't we? We knew everything we needed to know about each other from the very first moment we set eyes on one another, now didn't we, sugar plum?'

She tried surreptitiously to kick his shin but only succeeded in stumbling against him so that the length of her body was pressed uneasily against the length of his. Oh, dear. She was beginning to shake now. Desire licked at her like flames. She was being martyred here in her parents' front room on the pink, deep-pile carpet for the sake of her parents' feelings, and had it not been quite so delicious it wouldn't have been so absolutely dreadful.

He rested his chin on her head and made little circles on her neck with his thumb. It was as much as she could do not to moan out loud.

'Mr Houndsworth,' he murmured throatily, exactly as if he were profoundly moved by the proximity of the woman he loved, 'there's a carrier bag with a bottle of champagne in it at the side of my chair. Perhaps you'd like to do the honours?'

'Come on, Dad,' whispered her mother loudly. 'Let's give the young couple a few moments to themselves.'

Leon timed it perfectly. Just as they made for the door but before they were out of the room, he pressed his mouth hungrily to hers as if he couldn't wait another moment.

The instant the door clicked closed, Livvy dragged her mouth free of his—but it was already far too late. She had tasted his mouth and it was doing things to her which she badly resented. Shivering, she fought free of his arms, scurrying to the far side of the room and whispering fiercely, 'What the hell do you think you're up to, Leon Roche?'

He ran his tongue over his lips, letting a slow smile break across his face. Then he said, 'You said you wouldn't deceive them so I decided to do it for you.'

'You swine!' she returned through clenched teeth. 'I could kill you for that!'

He shrugged. 'For kissing you? Isn't that carrying things rather far? After all, it was a very nice kiss. I'm glad circumstances forced me to go back on my word and do it again.'

'Oh, shut up.' She scowled ferociously. 'I don't believe this! How could you do such a thing?'

He shook his head. 'Me? That's easy. I'm totally unscrupulous, Livvy. You're the one with principles, remember?'

She hugged her arms across her chest, hoping to quell the throbbing sensations which persisted even though contact had been broken. The trouble was, he was so outrageously attractive that even watching him across the room was turning her on. 'I hate you,' she wailed.

He pulled a wry face. 'Do you? Should I believe you? You're not as honest as you like to make out.'

'What do you mean now, you . . . you viper?'

'Well, you could have contradicted me in front of your parents, but you didn't. In other words, you were quite ready to deceive them after all.'

'Only because I changed my mind about marrying you on the drive down,' she hissed. 'Once I got here I was presented with a *fait accompli*. It seemed less hurtful to them to go along with your version of events than to tell the absolute truth.' She gave a bitter laugh. 'And anyway, if I had told the truth after you'd told them a pack of lies they would have fought tooth and nail to stop me marrying you, because they would have seen with their own eyes what a consummate liar and absolute charlatan you are. Once the deception had started it was the only thing I could do. You should be grateful to me.'

He walked slowly towards her. 'Really?' he growled sceptically, advancing a little more swiftly. She cowered back against the frilled Austrian blind. Mirth danced in his eyes. And then he paused and glanced towards the door. 'Get back into position quickly,' he commanded. 'I just heard the cork pop. They could be back at any moment with the glasses.' And so saying he wrapped his arms around her and covered his mouth with hers and kissed her all over again. His tongue was rapacious, delving between her lips and battling with her teeth until they parted for him. She waited until her parents were right inside the room and then bit hard. His fingers tightened against her upper arms, but that was the only sign he gave of the extreme pain she was sure she must have caused him. Very gently and very tenderly, and with lots of little delicate parting kisses, he let his mouth disengage from her mouth and then travel across her nose and her eyelids and her forehead.

'Love...' sighed her mother ecstatically. 'Now come on you two—tear yourselves away from each other and lets drink a toast. After all, you'll be married by this time next week. You'll have all the time in the world for canoodling then.'

'Next week?' muttered Livvy weakly.

'Thursday,' murmured Leon soothingly. 'I've sorted out a special licence. We'll have to get moving with the invitations.'

'No!' returned Livvy sharply, her mind beginning to focus at last. Two could play at this game. 'No, Leon,' she continued in a syrupy voice. 'You promised me, remember...? Just you and me. Remember?'

'And your parents as witnesses, sweetheart?'

'Er... yes. Of course. Just Mum and Dad as witnesses. It'll be so much more romantic that way; you'll see. And the other thing you promised, piglet, darling, was that we shouldn't see each other again until that special moment when we take our vows. I'll miss you like crazy, and I know you feel the same. But it'll be so much more romantic, won't it? So drink up your champagne. The next time we drink champagne together we'll be man and wife!'

Livvy spent the next week in a state of total bemusement. Scarcely a minute passed in which she didn't think of Leon Roche with poison in her heart. And yet, much as she yearned to thwart him, she *had* to go along with the plan. It just didn't make sense not to. She threw herself into her work with a fresh intensity which, ironically, she was now able to do as her parents were absolutely insistent that she shouldn't help them in the shop.

'Oh, no, Livvy,' they warned. 'Your artwork is much more important. Leon says it's quite remarkable. And we can always pay a girl to come in and help if we need anyone.'

She dressed for her wedding with more than usual care. So far she'd dressed with Major Fox, a serious dis-

cussion and a showdown in the office in mind. Today
Leon was going to get the genuine article—Livvy as she
liked to look—and she couldn't wait to see his face when
he clapped eyes on her.

'You can't go and get married dressed like that!' wailed
her mother when Livvy was ready. 'You look like a
gypsy! Why wouldn't you let your dad and me buy you
a proper dress? Oh, Livvy! And especially when you've
got all that lovely stuff in your wardrobe from my
catalogue...'

'Mum, he loves me for what I am. I promise it'll be
all right.'

'Well, at least let me stop off and get you some
flowers.'

'Mum, we've been through all this before. This is the
wedding of my dreams. I've always wanted it to be very
quiet and ordinary. I think it's more romantic.'

Her mother, regally decked out in cerise silk with
matching hat, sighed and bit her tongue. 'Well, at least
you're getting married,' she muttered finally. 'Which is
more than plenty of young women do these days. Now
hurry up. The white Rolls-Royce is waiting. It's a
surprise.'

'Oh, Mum.' Livvy's eyes filled with tears. How could
Leon do this to her parents? It was so cruel... 'That's
a lovely idea. And I do appreciate it. But the thing is,
I'll need my own car with me.'

'But you'll be a married woman. Leon will drive you
everywhere.'

'But when Leon's at work I'll need to be able to get
around. Leon understands that I'll need to keep some
independence.'

'Livvy! You can't go to your own wedding in that
old wreck!'

'Look, you and Dad use the Rolls. I'll drive up to London myself. And I promise I won't park near the register office. No one will see the Mini.'

She saw his car parked illegally outside the London register office as she strode up the sun-washed street, her hair tumbling free over her shoulders, her rich blue and pink patchwork silk waistcoat, crusted with richly coloured padded embroidery, vivid in the sun. The tiny bells in her earrings, ornate and hanging almost to her shoulders, shivered and tinkled as she moved, keeping time with the swoosh of her antique-pleated silk skirt which brushed against her bare legs. On her feet she wore flat, tooled-leather sandals. No doubt he'd be wearing a conventional dark suit and those Italian leather shoes of his. Ha!

The door of his car eased open as she approached. She lowered her eyes and tried to quash her gleeful smile. When she risked looking up again he was standing on the kerb, stretching and yawning, looking disgustingly relaxed in black jeans and a white T-shirt.

'Hi...' he drawled.

She frowned, looking him up and down. 'Is that what you consider suitable garb for a wedding?'

One of his lazy smiles broke slowly across his features. Her stomach lurched. How on earth had he come to have such blue eyes when his skin and hair and eyelashes were so stunningly dark? He dazzled her. Every time she looked into his eyes he dazzled her... His shoulders moved sinuously as he eased out his muscles. 'I consulted with your mother——'

'And that's another thing. My poor parents are——'

'Are inside waiting, and very happy. They're going straight from here to Heathrow to be flown out to join the QE2.'

'What? But they haven't any luggage! And the shop...?'

'The luggage problem has been taken care of. And your brother will be running the shop. His long vacation has started, after all.'

'My *brother*?' she echoed in disbelief. Ian hadn't set foot in the shop for years. Doctors-to-be, in his opinion, didn't weigh carrots.

'I had a word with him on the phone.'

'Well, OK, but what about the dinners, then? You see, there are these two old ladies down the road and every day Mum——'

'I know. Your brother will be taking care of them too.'

'Ian?'

'Ian's going to be a doctor one of these days with hundreds of old ladies as patients. He could see that it made sense to study the type early on in his training.'

'Even so——'

'Ian is your parents' child too,' Leon interrupted witheringly.

'So you took advantage of the fact that he's been brought up with a conscience to trick him?'

'Livvy, don't you want your parents to have the holiday of a lifetime? Or your brother to have the chance to improve his bedside manner?'

'Well, yes, of course I do.'

'So what's the problem now?'

'Oh, nothing,' she said irritably. 'Come on. Let's go in.'

But he shook his head, closing the car door and sauntering across to the wall of the red-brick building and leaning against it, his arms folded one across the other and his long legs crossed at the ankles. 'The last lot haven't come out yet and they've got six bridesmaids. I don't fancy getting stuck in there with them. We'll wait here until they appear.'

Stiffly she came to stand next to him, her back against the wall, ensuring that there was plenty of space between them and wishing that she'd worn a blouse beneath the waistcoat. But it had promised from the start to be such a hot day—and anyway the outfit looked so much better without...

'You look good,' he said as if he'd been reading her mind. But she couldn't help noticing that as he spoke he was looking outwards at the sun rather than at her.

'Pardon?'

'Mmm. I wouldn't have thought sharp colours would have suited you with all that coppery colour in your hair. But they do. Maybe it's because your skin isn't pale.'

Livvy touched her fingers to one of her prominent cheekbones. Her colour, she had to admit, was higher than was usual with auburn hair. She glanced down at the saturated blue of her skirt where it lay against the pale gold of her calf but said nothing in reply.

'Did you make that outfit yourself? I've never seen anything like it before.'

'I chose the fabrics and did the embroidery,' she muttered. 'A friend made it.'

'Ah-ha... One of those friends I'm not likely to bump into in the Street Café?'

Livvy thought of her friend Cassie and sighed. She probably lunched there every day lately. Very little in this world could be relied upon, it seemed—least of all the pit of her stomach, which was reacting to him quite shamelessly.

He looked down at his watch, wafer-thin platinum half buried beneath the dark hairs on his wrist, and reminding her all too vividly of the fine dark hairs which sat close to his skin, tapering down to his navel. She shivered.

She dared not look up at the thick black hair of his head, nor at the smooth, strong hairs of his eyebrows, nor at the wiry hairs visible at the neck of his T-shirt, for fear of what the sight might do to her already scorching insides.

'We'll have a celebratory lunch at the Golden Nightingale and then I thought——'

'And then I have work to do,' Livvy bit out. 'I can't afford to waste time while I'm in London. I'll play the part during lunch, but after that I'm off to the university library. You can do what you like.'

He smiled broadly. 'That's not a very romantic way to spend your wedding-day.'

'Golden Nightingale...' she muttered witheringly. The wretched place had been recently built on a prestigious site and billed as London's most romantic hotel. Most expensive, more like...

He yawned. 'Never mind. It suits me fine. As long as you don't do anything which will draw attention to the fact that our marriage is not all it might be presumed to be, there's no problem. I can spend the afternoon at Katya's, after all. She's always willing.'

Jealous? Oh, no. It couldn't be jealousy she was feeling, because there could be no possible reason for it. It was *disgust*. That was what it was. 'And single, I take it?' she said coldly.

'And single,' he agreed, narrowing his eyes and regarding her keenly. Then he pressed his lips into a thin smile. 'I'll have to look in at my office for ten minutes before we go down to Herefordshire. Something rather critical blew up this morning. I'll see you there at five, ready to drive you down to Purten End.'

She risked a wary glance in his direction. 'If you give me the keys to the house I can go on ahead.'

One corner of one eyebrow lifted fractionally. 'No fear,' he said very softly and very dangerously. 'I'm not letting you loose in that place until we've established the ground rules. You can come with me. I'll carry you over the threshold myself and choose exactly where to set you down. In the eyes of the world, Livvy, we're a pair of love-soaked newly-weds. We can be as unconventional as we like in the way we go about things—but we *do* have to go about them. Remember that.'

Livvy's heart began to thunder, but before she could work herself up to respond a gaggle of green brides-maids burst out of the door beside them in a shower of confetti. Leon grasped her arm firmly and hustled her past a bulging bride swathed in white satin, through a horde of cheering guests and into the silence of the office beyond.

When she next looked at him her breath caught in her throat. Each lustrous black curl housed pastel fragments of confetti, and both the olive skin of his brow and the strong line of his jaw were gilded with glitter which one of the guests must have thrown. Had she been asked she would have said that throwing glitter at a wedding was a tacky thing to do—and yet the effect was absolutely stunning. He seemed scarcely human, shining gold along the hard planes of his face, stardust glinting from the swell of his lower lip. Inside she weakened. Why on earth did she want to fight this man?

He looked at her then and smiled. 'You're shining,' he said. His voice was deep and rich, resonating in the quiet of the big room. 'You look gorgeous, Livvy. Edible. Quite, quite beautiful.'

She touched the tip of her tongue to her lower lip and realised that she, too, was dusted in gold. Shaken, she lowered her eyes. As she stood beside him, looking at him, hearing his voice saying such a thing to her, her heart began to sing, and the sound frightened her. Livvy had always hoped that one day she would marry someone for real. If ever that day came she would once again find herself standing beside her groom, waiting. Would the sight of the man she loved move her as much as the sight of Leon, speckled with tawdry glitter, had done? Would she feel as good, as proud, as joyous as she had in that fleeting moment when he'd spoken?

Fearfully she fixed her eyes on the registrar who was beckoning her parents forward and speaking of matrimony.

Leon's arm came possessively around Livvy's shoulder. Then he looked down at her. 'Ready?' he murmured, his voice deep and compelling. He looked into her eyes and for once his eyes seemed not blue but black, reflective and dark. Unable to speak she nodded slowly, waiting for the proceedings to proceed.

When it got to the exchange of rings bit, Leon's eyes crinkled with amusement and he said calmly to her, 'I don't actually have a ring. And I'm sure you don't, either, do you?'

She unknotted her clenched fists and breathed out, shaking her head wordlessly. But then he said, 'So I'll give you a medal instead,' and he bent over her and attached a diamond broach to her waistcoat, just over her heart, slipping his fingers under the neck-edge to hold the cloth taut. She almost screamed out loud. Why hadn't she worn a blouse? His smooth fingernails pressed against the swell of her breast while his other hand deftly fastened the pin.

Livvy tried to unfocus her eyes, which were gazing almost hungrily at the relaxed curve of his mouth, just inches away from her own. When he straightened up and she looked down at the brooch, small and pretty, shaped like a crescent moon, it seemed to wink knowingly at her. She blushed fiercely.

'You may kiss the bride if you wish, sir,' came the congratulatory tones of the registrar's voice at last.

'Good,' he said drily. Then he looked tauntingly at Livvy and said, 'It'll be all the better for having waited a week. Won't it, darling?'

Panicked, she stood on tiptoe and brushed her lips swiftly against his before stepping back out of harm's way.

'Much better,' he conceded wryly, his mouth close to her ear. 'Quite painless in fact.'

Guiltily she recalled biting his tongue.

'You're managing very well, darling,' he murmured, guiding her towards the register. 'You've obviously got over your pre-wedding nerves. Keep going.'

She nodded weakly, her mossy-green eyes round and bright. Anxiously she hurried forward to sign whatever it was they had to sign, watching Leon's bold, confusing script run confidently from the tip of the pen before snatching it from him and adding her own, neat, upright signature.

When it was over Leon put his arm around her and guided both her and her parents out into the sunshine. The white Rolls-Royce was waiting, a uniformed chauffeur holding the door wide.

'Now, you're to enjoy every minute of the cruise. You'll be met at the airport and taken to Bloomingdale's before you join the ship. Have fun with those gold cards—please. I want you to enjoy everything to the full, as a special thank-you for giving me the best present I've ever had.' And he hugged Livvy so tightly she couldn't breathe.

'Oh, Mr Roche...Leon...' her mother began huskily. But he silenced her with a shake of his head and dazzled them both with a smile.

As the portly couple clambered into the car a green bridesmaid slipped out of a group photograph and shook a box of confetti over them. 'Be good!' the girl cried happily. Tears sprang to Livvy's eyes as she watched her parents, as happy as any newly-weds and undoubtedly good, slip out of sight. Her heart felt like lead.

She walked away from him into a patch of sun-baked pavement. 'What happens now?' she said nervously, studiously avoiding looking over her shoulder at him as she spoke.

'We're off to the hotel.'

Her skin prickled and she felt quite faint. She glanced down at the brooch. 'Why did you give me this?'

'It reminded me of the way you sparkled the first day you came to see me,' he drawled, tongue-in-cheek.

'I was studying your muscles,' she muttered in response.

'Yeah...so you said.' He sounded distinctly sceptical. Then he added, 'I thought it was more honest than a ring.'

'I don't like deceit,' she said stiffly.

'It's a bit late to worry about that. Anyway, the characters in your wonderfully honest and truthful love story practised their deceit in church. Isn't that worse?'

Livvy's face flamed. She bit down on her lower lip. 'I'll unpin it and give it back...hang on.' And her fingers began to fumble with the fastening.

His hand came over her shoulder to stay her shaking fingers. 'There's no need.'

Oh, lord, why did he have to touch her? Desire danced in her blood. 'But there is, Leon! If it was just meant as a ruse——'

'It was also meant as a gift,' he said, and behind the soft, sunny, afternoon tenor of his voice she detected an icy and distinctly nocturnal determination.

'Well . . . if you say so . . .'

'I do.'

She dug her toes downwards into the soles of her sandals. Although she had her back to him, she was screamingly aware of the weight of his hand on her bare skin, not to mention his powerful frame just inches from her back. God, this was getting worse by the minute. 'OK,' she croaked.

His fingers tightened against her flesh. 'Let's hope we both get what we want from this marriage, eh, Livvy?' His voice floated menacingly among the loose waves of her hair.

'Uh-huh . . .' she ventured. There was a tightness about every sound she made which announced the condition of her flesh more coherently than any moan of desire.

He drew her closer to him so that she was forced to take an uneasy step backwards. 'Still not tempted, Livvy?' he asked softly.

She wasn't near enough to him for their bodies to be touching, but none the less her shoulder-blades almost met behind her as a great wash of desire shuddered through her. 'No,' she snapped determinedly. 'Not a bit.'

'Liar.'

He took his hands off her shoulders and stepped back.

She turned and looked at him.

'Come on,' he said crisply. 'Get into my car quickly before a traffic warden turns up.'

CHAPTER SIX

LIVVY allowed herself to be led in through the imposing foyer of the Golden Nightingale. 'Will they let you eat here without a tie?' she whispered.

He tilted his head to one side. 'We'll eat in the honeymoon suite. I don't think they'll care what I'm wearing up there.'

'Oh... But I thought the point of this meal was to flaunt ourselves?'

'Did you?'

'Well, of course I did. After all, we're hardly going to make use of the...um...facilities, are we?'

'It doesn't matter,' he teased. 'I can afford it.'

Livvy sighed crossly. But she didn't argue the point.

He touched her elbow. 'Come on. Let's go into the lounge and have an aperitif. We can flaunt ourselves there for ten minutes, if that's what you want.'

'Of course it isn't what I want,' she sighed.

'You want to go straight to the honeymoon suite?'

Livvy gave a weak groan. 'How do you do it? I can't keep up with you... Come on. Let's have that drink. Perhaps it will fortify me.'

Leon gave an amused growl and led her through into the lounge, where he seated her with her back to the window, facing the door. 'There. Flaunt away. Everyone should get an excellent view of you there.'

And they did. Time after time as the glass doors swung open, eyes fixed themselves admiringly on Livvy. Even the waiter seemed transfixed by her. 'This is horrible,' she muttered. 'Everybody's looking at us. Why? Is it because we're so casually dressed?'

'*You're* not,' he said. 'You're beautifully dressed.'

'We-ell . . . yes, but I'm not dressed the way they are.'

'Which simply makes you all the more stunning in their eyes.'

She eyed him uncertainly. 'I've worn this before. I've never attracted half this attention.'

'Perhaps it's the change of situation?'

'You mean because I'm with you?'

His smile widened. 'No. I mean because you're rubbing shoulders with people who can afford to dress exactly as they choose down to the last coat button. They're judging you by their own standards. They aren't thinking, How clever of Livvy to make herself something so beautiful. They're thinking, Which couturier dressed that woman? And how do I get a piece of the action for myself? Still, it was very kind of you to assume that it was on my account that you were attracting all this attention. But then, we do make the perfect couple, don't we, Livvy?'

'Oh, be quiet.'

To which he declined to reply; but it didn't feel like a triumph.

They were sipping in silence when yet another well-dressed man came in through the glass doors and did a double take. This one did a triple take, though, stopped, and then strode purposefully towards them. He was a handsome man in his mid-sixties, with white hair and an engaging smile.

'Damn it,' muttered Leon under his breath as the man approached. Then he stood up. 'Richard . . . good to see you,' and he held out his hand towards the older man.

'Leon, you devil!' growled the newcomer, grasping Leon's hand warmly. 'I thought you were getting married today?'

'I have, Richard. Indeed I have. Let me present you to my brand-new wife—Olivia Roche. Livvy, this is Sir Richard Gallagher.'

'Oh...' Livvy sent up a modest little smile. Help! She hadn't counted on meeting the man quite so soon. She hadn't worked out her strategy yet. 'Um... how do you do?' she stalled, holding her hand limply towards him.

He took it in both of his and pressed it to his mouth. 'My dear!' he exclaimed, smiling into her eyes. 'What a delight! I've heard a great deal about you—and all of it quite formidable. I'm told that you're the only woman alive capable of taming this husband of yours.'

Livvy's green eyes widened with alarm. She was going to have to say something to the point now, but what should it be? 'Oh. Well...I...um...I certainly hope so,' she replied earnestly. 'I can assure you that that's very much my intention, Mr...um...Sir Richard. I have very high ideals where marriage is concerned. And everything else, actually. And Leon and I plan to—er—share everything,' she finished lamely.

Sir Richard nodded approvingly then freed her hand and grinned at Leon. 'Just married, eh?' he said wryly, eyeing his T-shirt and jeans.

'Fresh from the ceremony,' admitted Leon with a humorous smile.

Then Sir Richard turned back to Livvy and wagged a finger at her. 'Don't let this scoundrel call all the shots.' He leaned forward and peered at her brooch. 'Oh, yes. Very nice. No need to ask if I can see the ring, because there won't be one.'

'Richard, have you no tact?' asked Leon amiably, slapping the older man on the shoulder. 'We've just tied the knot. Livvy doesn't want to spend the first few hours of married life making small talk with an old codger like you. We'll be dining with you next week to celebrate the merger, anyhow. Time enough for all your ramblings then. Now clear off, there's a good chap!'

Richard Gallagher straightened up and barked out a resilient laugh. 'Point taken,' he said, turning to go. And then he looked back over his shoulder at Livvy and said confidingly, 'Start as you mean to go on, my dear. OK?'

The moment he was out of earshot Livvy frowned at Leon. 'What did he mean, start as you mean to go on? And how did he know that I had a brooch instead of a ring?'

Leon shrugged. 'It's traditional in my family. My father gave my mother one on their wedding-day.'

'Oh.' Livvy looked down at the beautiful little crescent of diamonds and felt her heart unaccountably sink. 'Oh. So you knew that *he'd* know and so you...uh...' Her voice tailed away. She actually sounded disappointed and she really didn't want to have to try explaining to him why. Or to herself for that matter. 'Can we get on with this meal?' she said instead.

Leon responded by getting to his feet and taking her hand. Silently he led her out of the carpeted bar into the lift.

The suite was astonishing. It was decorated entirely in silver and white, contained a heart-shaped water bed with silvery satin sheets, and was decked with red roses. It was horribly tasteless and yet quite deliciously sumptuous. Her mother would have loved it.

Huge windows gave on to a balcony overlooking one of London's leafiest parks. A silver table and chairs was set out on the balcony, furnished with rosebuds and champagne. Leon seated her then picked up a silver phone and told Room Service that he was ready.

Moments later a battalion of waiters arrived with oysters and caviare and truffles and smoked salmon, yet more flowers and, to Livvy's open-mouthed amazement, the food was accompanied by a kilted piper playing 'Scotland the Brave'. In their wake followed a stream of bellhops laden with gaily packaged parcels.

When they had gone she stared at him round-eyed in amazement. 'What was all that about?'

He chuckled. 'Did you like it?'

'We-ell...' What on earth could she say to that?

'Of course you didn't! You weren't meant to. What you were meant to do is get a taste for the extraordinary things money can buy. Now tell me, Livvy, how do you think Rosamund would have reacted?'

'She would have...' She looked wonderingly at the stack of gifts. 'Well, she would have been bound to be pleased in a way,' she admitted ruefully. 'Of course, she wouldn't have sold her soul for a heap of presents, but I do think she must have been pleased.'

Leon blazed a smile at her. 'Open some.'

Guardedly she unwrapped first a small packet. It was a gold choker. And then a large packet. It was a taffeta ballgown. And then a tiny packet which proved to be car keys.

He nodded at the keys. 'You can't pick that up till next week, I'm afraid. I'm having it customised.'

Her cheeks flushed crimson. 'I can't take all this! It wasn't part of the deal.'

'Open some more.'

Her heart thudding dully, she opened several medium-sized packages. Silk nightwear. A little green cocktail dress the same colour as her eyes. Gold leather shoes.

'I...I'm flabbergasted,' she admitted. 'Why?'

'You're my wife.'

'Oh . . . I see.' Of course, she would need stuff like this when she was seen with him in public. Even so, Livvy was stunned. She really didn't know what to make of it. She fingered the blue taffeta of the ballgown. It was truly beautiful. She was moved. She had to admit it to herself. She really was.

'I . . .' She held up the cocktail dress which bore a designer label. 'It's even my size!' she exclaimed.

'Oh, good.'

'How did you know what size I was?'

'Well, I sort of described you to a friend of mine. She's about the same height as you are but a bit rounder.'

Livvy put the dress down on the pile of crumpled wrapping paper and chewed worriedly at the corner of her mouth. She wasn't jealous, because that wouldn't make sense. But something jabbed and dug at the pit of her stomach none the less. Guilt, she decided. 'I don't want all this stuff, Leon,' she said cagily. 'I really don't.'

'Why?'

She sighed. During the past week she had given a great deal of thought to the matter of civilising Leon Roche. She had considered shoving articles about unemployment under his nose and playing him classical music, but she couldn't exactly see such tactics having any effect. In the end she'd decided that the only solution was to use her own behaviour as an example. If she stuck to her principles absolutely in every facet of her life perhaps she could prove to him that there was another way to live. A civilised way.

'You like them, though?' he persisted.

'Oh, yes. I'm not without taste, even if this stuff isn't quite my usual style. They're all . . . very nice.'

'So what's the problem? You've admitted that Rosamund would have enjoyed being showered with gifts, after all.'

'Well, yes. But actually, even though Rosamund ate posh food and wore posh clothes, she spent the six months walking the countryside, dispensing charity. Which must mean that she didn't turn into a grand lady overnight. Um...she just went on being herself. I...I...um... Look, I suppose I'm prepared to keep these things as part of my new public persona, but I'm not impressed by them as such, and I don't really want them and I won't use them except when I'm on view as your wife.'

He regarded her impassively. 'Well, that's fine. To be honest, I was surprised you even opened them.'

'Oh.'

He smiled at her. 'We're getting on much better since we got married, don't you think? Marriage must suit you. I think you're moving in the right direction already, Livvy.' Then he put his elbows on the table, cupped his chin in his hands and looked mockingly into her eyes. 'Now, would you like some money to give to charity, too? I can arrange a bank account for you and you can walk about the country dispensing largesse as you see fit.'

'No!'

'You mean you wouldn't like some money to give to charity?'

'Well, yes...of course I would. But I mean... Oh, you know... The thing is...uh...' Livvy closed her eyes. 'The thing is, well, you know, the widow's mite and all that...'

'You mean you'd rather give small amounts of your own money to charity than large amounts of mine?'

'I...yes, I suppose so. I mean no, not really...I...' She sighed helplessly, opening her worried eyes.

'If you give small amounts of your own money it won't do much good to the people you give it to, of course, but it'll make you feel terrific. On the other hand if you hand out large amounts of my money——'

'Look, Leon, I haven't had a chance to sort my thoughts out yet. There's quite a profound philosophic point buried in there somewhere, and it's only ten minutes since I had a Scotsman blowing the bagpipes in my ear. Can we leave this discussion till a later date?'

He frowned as if he was concentrating very hard. 'Rosamund would have given out large amounts of her husband's money, I think. Because she wouldn't have had any of her own to give, would she? Now, does that make her more principled than you or less?'

'I... Leon, can we leave this discussion till later, please?'

His mouth curled with amusement and his eyes sparked wickedly. 'But I thought you wanted to share your ideals not just with Rosamund but with *me*, Livvy?' And then he picked up an oyster shell and tipped the contents languorously into his mouth.

Oh, lord, this was dreadful. It was as if she were watching his mouth in cinematic close-up; every curve and line; the glimpse of those perfect, ivory teeth; the still gilded fullness of his lower lip; the opalescent shell and the moist, glistening curves of the reputedly aphrodisiac oyster. Temptation whispered, silver and white, in the summer's breeze. Oh, dear. She wasn't succumbing, was she? That wasn't the reason why they seemed to be getting on a little better, was it? She swallowed hard, then shakily she stood up. 'Look, I've got to go,' she blurted out. 'I've got things to do. I... I told you before... I've got to work.'

'Stay for half an hour,' he cajoled beguilingly.

'Half an hour?' she squeaked. Anything could happen in half an hour! She glanced at the pile of gifts. 'I...I need time to think. I've got to go.'

'You're not tempted by any chance, are you, Livvy? Tempted by this wanton display of power and wealth?'

She shook her head furiously. 'Oh, no...' she denied, and then, to prove it, hurried to the door. 'I'll...um...catch up with you later,' she said in a voice which was tight with strain. 'I have important work to be getting on with. Five, you said? At your office?'

'Five,' he confirmed genially. 'I'll see you then...'

At five o'clock she presented herself to his secretary, feeling dusty and tired after an afternoon spent in libraries poring over history books. His voice set the intercom trembling. 'Tell her she'll have to wait, Lulu. Make her a cup of coffee and offer her a seat and keep her sweet.'

The secretary, eighteenish and slender, turned to Livvy and said, 'Mr Roche apologises but——'

'He didn't apologise, actually,' Livvy sighed, plonking herself on an office chair. 'I was standing right next to you and I heard every word. And the answer's yes, I'd love a cup. No sugar.'

'He's in a bad mood,' the secretary whispered confidingly. 'He's had one of those days,' and then she clapped her hand to her mouth guiltily. 'I mean, I'm sure it's the happiest day of his life really and he's only been here for ten minutes... It's just that there were a few crisisy things to sort out when he arrived.'

'Don't worry. Leon and I understand each other,' Livvy replied. Well, it was half true; she didn't understand him, but he certainly seemed to understand her.

In the twenty minutes it took her to consume two cups of coffee the secretary revealed that her name was Gina but Mr Roche called her Lulu—she didn't know why—and that she had terrible trouble getting shoes to fit as she had such small bones. 'Gosh,' replied Livvy. Then Gina asked coyly whether it had been a nice wedding and Livvy said that yes, on balance it had, but just saying it set her teeth on edge. Because in a funny sort of way it had been a wonderful wedding—but she could hardly say *that*, now could she?

When Leon finally appeared, mysteriously changed into a charcoal suit, a crisp white shirt with a purple mottled tie and shiny Italian shoes, she sighed with relief. There was so much less of him a view in a suit than in T-shirt and jeans. He'd got rid of the glitter too, thank goodness.

'I've put my Mini in the car park behind the building,' she said briskly. 'All my luggage is in it. Shall I follow you down?'

He frowned. 'Why did you do that? I mean, couldn't you have left your stuff in Bristol and shifted it later?'

'Why? What difference does it make to you?'

'I'm hot and tired. I'd like to get down to the country as fast as possible.'

'Well? Don't let me detain you. Drive down to Purten End as fast as you like. I'll follow in my car.'

Irritation flashed across his face. 'I can get one of the security staff to move your junk into my car... It won't take long,' he countered dismissively.

'But if you do that then I'll be stuck in Herefordshire without a car.'

'So? I'll get a driver to bring it down in the next few days. Anyway, you'll have the new one next week.'

'Why should I want to be stuck even for that short a time, Leon?' she replied crossly.

He looked at her with mind-blowing coldness. Then he shrugged. 'OK. Suit yourself.' And with that he strode across to his swish car, got in and drove off.

As she fidgeted with her own car keys she couldn't help feeling aggrieved. Was it her fault that he'd had a hard day? It appeared that he was the sort of man who'd pick on anything to make a scene when he was in the wrong sort of mood. Well, thank goodness he wasn't really her husband. Imagine being married to someone as bad-tempered as that.

When she arrived at last at Purten End it was to find his car parked in the shade of a chestnut tree on the cobbled courtyard.

To her annoyance the house seemed very empty, and she had to ring the bell twice before Leon appeared around the side of the house, wearing white shorts and a white polo shirt. He had a white sweatband around one wrist and a good deal of perspiration coating his olive skin to justify its existence. He had a tennis racket in one hand.

'Livvy... At last,' he said and his eyes shone with sardonic amusement.

She felt almost sick with desire at the sight of him. 'At last? How long have you been here?'

'I don't know. Long enough to have taken a quick shower and knocked a few balls against the wall in the orchard.'

Livvy's temper flickered dangerously. 'You must have broken the speed limit to have got here so soon,' she said coldly. 'It's a wonder you still have a licence.'

'And it's a wonder you still have any teeth,' he returned, keeping his firmly clenched.

Livvy glanced away from his dazzling blue eyes, ignoring his remark. 'Don't you know that the wall in the orchard is for the benefit of the espaliered fruit trees, not for your sporting entertainment? Mrs Major Fox devoted years to the peaches.'

The last vestiges of amusement shrivelled in Leon's eyes as she spoke. He shook his head slowly. 'Come with me...' He sighed bitterly. 'Let me show you the orchard as it is now.' And with that he held out one of his big square hands to her.

Livvy's stomach somersaulted.

'What? You mean you've spoiled that lovely orchard already?' she bit out, so angry with herself that she could choke. 'How many weeks have you been living here, Leon? Two? Three? How long does it take a man like you to turn a wonderful old Elizabethan house into a multi-storey car park?'

'Oh, for God's sake, Livvy, stop being so bloody dreary. What the hell is the matter with you? You come from a nice family. You've never wanted for anything in your life. You're beautiful and talented... And here you are in a gorgeous corner of England early on a summer's evening and all you can do is snipe. You're a spoiled, sour-minded little bitch.'

'I'm not! I'm just furious because——'

'Because my car goes faster than your car? I'm not a reckless driver, Livvy, but the car is powerful enough to take good advantage of motorway driving. I usually make good time on long journeys. On the other hand, I doubt I find it as easy to park or to nip around town as you do in your Mini. Count your blessings, can't you, instead of wasting all your energy in being critical?'

'That's not what I'm doing!' she complained crossly.

'Isn't it?' And he looked her up and down with cold disdain. Then he sighed heavily, strolled over to the door, leant his racket against the warm bricks, extracted some keys from his shorts pocket and opened the door into the hall.

Livvy followed him in. He strode swiftly across the hall, and then stopped dead in his tracks. She saw his shoulders swell and then drop as he took in and released a deep breath. Then he turned to face her, the muscles of his face tightly controlled. 'Why don't I briefly show you around, and then perhaps we can both get changed and go out for a meal? We've got quite a lot to settle one way or another, and it would be a pleasure to do it over a few glasses of wine and with a good meal inside us, don't you think? I'm sure you've had as long and tiring a day as I have.'

She could see that he was battling with his own instincts in order to avoid a blazing row. She ought to have been pleased, but her stupid body was far too aware of him for her to feel anything but dangerously unsettled. She ignored the white flag. 'Visit a restaurant with you? No, thank you. I've tried it already and it's not an experience I'm eager to repeat. Anyway, I've brought my own groceries. If you'll just show me which cupboard in the kitchen I can consider mine I'll see to my own meal.'

And then his big fists clenched very hard and he stuck them on his hips, the muscles of his forearms rigid beneath the mantle of dark hair. His thighs were apart, his feet planted squarely on the polished boards as if ready for a fight. 'I very rarely make mistakes in life,' he said angrily. 'But you have to be my biggest error of judgement ever.'

This time when his hand came out towards her it didn't hesitate. He grasped her wrist painfully and pulled her towards him. She heard a small whimpering noise escape from her throat and every nerve in her body jumped to attention. This was it! He was going to kiss her again and she wasn't going to be able to resist. Panic flurried inside her.

He looked coldly into her wide eyes. 'Look at you!' he bit out scornfully. 'Your mouth is open, ready and waiting. Well, I'm sorry to disappoint you, little girl, but I've no intention of kissing you. I merely wanted to show you the facilities.' And with that he began to walk, pulling her along behind him.

As she scuttled down the corridor at his side, blinking furiously, she felt ready to die of mortification. Matters were not helped when he threw open a very heavy oak door to reveal the house's original kitchen, exactly as she remembered it and looking like something from a museum.

He pushed her in ahead of him, letting go of her arm as he did so. 'It's all yours, Livvy,' he said disdainfully. 'Luckily the house has two kitchens so you won't have to struggle with the difficulties of sharing a kitchen with an uncouth savage who might mangle your hands at any moment. There's a complete set of copper pans hanging from the ceiling, and plenty of firewood waiting to be gathered in the woods. All you need now to roast your own ox is a packet of firelighters and a dog.'

And with that he turned on his heel and strode away.

CHAPTER SEVEN

LIVVY, having not unpacked her alarm clock, slept until eight forty-five. She flung open her window to let in the morning, thereby giving herself a glimpse of the courtyard, where, to her dismay, she noted her car still stood all alone. He had departed the previous evening after cursorily introducing her to the bedroom she was to be allowed to use, her own antedeluvian bathroom and water closet and a small sitting-room with a black and white portable television, adding very forcefully that on no account was she to use any other rooms in the house. She had been heartily glad to see him go at the time—not the least because it meant that she'd been able to use his kitchen to heat up her ready-made tandoori chicken without losing face: the packaging had given cooking instructions for both conventional and microwave ovens, but had made no mention of spit-roasting over an open fire.

Now that day had dawned, however, she felt unaccountably lonely in the deserted house. She was making herself a comforting cup of tea in his kitchen when the phone rang. 'Hello?'

'Hi! That's Olivia speaking, isn't it?'

'Yes. That's right. Who are you?'

'Katya. We spoke once before. Remember?'

'Oh.' It would be hard, actually, to forget the velocity of that particular telephone voice. 'Er—I take it you want to speak to Leon?'

'Yes.'

'He's not available to come to the phone, I'm sorry.'

'Drat! Hasn't he had his breakfast yet? Honestly, he is a nuisance. He doesn't do it because he's grumpy in the mornings, you know, but so that he has a little patch of the day in which other people aren't allowed to irritate him. Now, what do you think of that? It's selfish, isn't it?'

'Uh... Oh, yes. I suppose it is.'

'Damn right it is. Anyway, tell him that it's me and that it's urgent. Tell him that he's got to make an exception for me.'

'I can't. He's not here.'

'Not there? But you *did* get married yesterday?'

'Yes. He drove down yesterday evening, but then he went back to London for the night.'

'Back to London? Really? How odd.' There was an unpleasant little silence. Livvy felt as if she was being accused of something. 'Well, he didn't come home to me. But if he didn't stay at Purten End either, then where did he spend the night...?'

'Katya, are you Leon's sister or something? I mean, are you related to him in some way?'

'Did you ask if I was his sister?' echoed Katya, her voice incredulous. And then, to Livvy's horror, the other woman put down the phone.

Livvy glared at the receiver, hot with indignation. Really, this was the absolute end. Livvy hadn't cared to speculate too much on Leon's other women, but she'd never had any doubt that there must be plenty of them. Katya she had merely supposed to be the single and willing woman of the moment. But it was a bit much for her to be expected to chat with her about the wedding less than twenty-four hours after the ceremony! OK, so she was his wife in name only... She didn't have any real claim on him at all. But even so...if she was expected to wear green cocktail dresses then surely he could be expected to give up his lecherous liaisons for six months.

Desperate to cool her blood, Livvy stormed to her bathroom. But when she turned on the bath taps no more than a trickle of rusty water emerged. The basin, whose taps had worked fine the previous evening, also managed only a small, wet cough. Undeterred, she gathered together her toilet things and stamped through the house, opening doors until she discovered a bathroom which looked extremely functional: Leon's, obviously. It had a modern suite—blindingly white, with stacks of red and black towels on white shelves, and a jet shower in one corner of the spacious room. Angrily she tore off her dressing-gown and nightdress, grabbed a bottle of Leon's shampoo and switched on the powerful shower full blast. This time water gushed out prolifically, drenching her from head to toe, pounding against her face so that she screwed up her eyes against the spray while she lathered the lemony shampoo into her hair.

She bared her teeth and grimaced into the shower-head, choking a little as hot water spurted between her teeth, spouting it back out again like a gargoyle. She found a tablet of soap on a wall-mounted magnet and rubbed it energetically over her skin. Finally she stumbled out of the spray and grabbed a towel, pressing it hard against her face and pushing it upwards so that it swept her wet hair back from her brow. Then she opened her eyes to discover that what she had assumed was the door of an airing cupboard—a flimsy, louvred structure—was itself open, and propped in the space was Leon Roche, his hair tousled, his jaw black and unshaven and his skin sleepy. He was naked as the day that he was born. But a lot bigger.

'How long have *you* been there?' she demanded in a strangled voice.

He smiled very slowly but said nothing.

Hastily she scuttled across the room towards the stack of towels, grabbed a huge red one, shook it open and draped it modestly across herself, keeping her back to him. She threw a black towel over her shoulder in his direction. He began to laugh then, a deep, resonant laugh which ran all over her skin like a hot, equatorial wind.

'Shut up,' she hissed. Surprisingly he fell silent. Unnerved, she risked a quick glance in his direction. He had wound the towel low about his hips—thank goodness—but his eyes were still laughing and his shoulders quaked with mirth.

'If you were a gentleman you'd have left the room the moment you saw I was in here.'

Still he didn't reply.

Briskly she marched over to the basin, took a glass from the shelf alongside and filled it with water. She held it out towards him, desperately struggling to keep her eyes off his virile form. 'Breakfast,' she announced tautly. 'Drink this and perhaps it will loosen your tongue.'

His eyes narrowed and he stopped laughing. 'Why don't you stop talking, Livvy, and get out of my bathroom and make yourself decent?' he asked in a voice which was low and gravelly and dangerous.

'I didn't ask you to burst in on me!' she exclaimed furiously.

'And I didn't ask you to use my bathroom. Far from it.'

'It's the only one with any water,' she snapped.

'Is it?'

'Well, it's the only one I could find which had any water worth speaking of. That one you gave me doesn't work properly. And anyhow, I didn't even know it was your bathroom.'

He let his eyes travel around the room. 'I would say there's fairly good presumptive evidence.'

'I bolted the door!'

'You didn't bolt the door to my room. What did you expect to happen?'

'Look. The thing is, I didn't know that that was a door too. It looks too trashy to be a proper door. Though I might have guessed *you* had it installed. It's very much your style.'

'Are you being honest, Livvy?' he asked coldly. 'Is this a genuine mistake?'

'Now look here,' she spat, closing her eyes and turning her head to one side to avoid staring at him. 'I didn't even know you were in the house. You marched out last night and I assumed you'd gone back to London. You took your car. And I checked this morning—it's not parked outside. I thought I had the house to myself.' She opened her eyes a crack, tipped her head back and surveyed him over her cheekbones, taking great care not to look below the level of his stubbly jaw. The dark triangular shadow of the hairs on his chest mysteriously seemed to impinge upon her inner eye none the less.

He studied her coolly for a moment. Then he ran his hands through his tousled curls and lowered his hooded lids as if to acknowledge the strength of her case. 'A genuine error in that case...' he conceded drily.

'And one which need only have lasted a split-second if you'd turned your back on me the moment you saw I was in here. Now for goodness' sake why don't you get out of here and let me finish my ablutions with some dignity?'

'I'm getting too much pleasure out of seeing you discomfited, that's why,' he owned.

'I'm not discomfited,' she lied crossly.

'Aren't you? I'm not sure that I believe you. Sometimes we give away more than we intend...' he replied.

'We had life models at college—of both sexes. You're no more than an anatomical exercise to me.'

'Liar,' he mouthed, but his mouth made no sound.

'I'm not!'

His eyebrows quirked but he said nothing.

'Silence again,' she observed acidly. 'Excellent. So you've remembered that you haven't had breakfast yet? Wonderful. The sound of your voice sets my teeth on edge at the best of times, let alone first thing in the morning.'

For a moment she thought she had won, because he still said nothing. But then he took a few steps towards her and very lightly put a mocking hand to the curve of her towel-swathed breasts. His thumb gently circled the hard peak of one nipple, which had been throbbing incessantly since she had clapped eyes on him lounging naked in the doorway.

Livvy jumped, then took a step backwards, glaring at him. 'What a nerve,' she accused. 'I suppose you think that proves something?'

Still he said nothing.

Flustered, she dropped her eyes, then spun on her heel as she realised where her own gaze had taken itself. She wasn't the only one whose towel revealed as much as it concealed and the knowledge frightened her. Frantically she began gathering her bits and pieces together, disconcerted beyond measure at his silence. 'I suppose,' she muttered bitterly, keeping her back to him, 'you think I ought to leap into bed with you just because *you* happen to feel like it? Well, it may interest you to know that I have principles which would absolutely forbid any such thing unless I was deeply in love with the person in question. So there.'

Naturally he didn't reply.

Clutching her things, she unbolted the door to the landing with a sharp flick of her wrist and scuttled back to her room.

Dressed in her own tight jeans and a loose green silk shirt under a multicoloured brocade waistcoat, she finally plucked up the courage to go downstairs and confront him again. Except, she realised with satisfaction, there needn't be any confrontation as long as she didn't trespass on his space. He'd set the rules hoping to catch her out, but all she had to do was obey them and he'd be stumped...

Fifteen minutes later he opened the door to her kitchen to find her in the early stages of boiling water over a tiny camp fire constructed in the middle of the enormous hearth. For the second time that morning she had the distinction of making him laugh. 'You've got spirit, Livvy, I have to grant you that,' he said. 'Where did you find the matches?'

She tucked her hair behind her ears before allowing herself to turn her head and look up at him piously. 'I take it you've had your breakfast already?'

'No.'

'In which case, to what do I owe the undoubted honour of yet another pre-breakfast conversation?'

'Rules are made to be broken. And I need to communicate with you and it's by far the simplest way.'

'Well, say what you have to say and then go,' she replied haughtily.

He gave her one of his lazy smiles and paused for an insolent moment while she turned back to her feeble little fire and began blowing on the pathetic flames. Her knees were cold from kneeling on the stone-flagged floor.

'I drove over to the Purten country club last night to eat,' he began. 'It's less than a mile from here—we're next-door neighbours as a matter of fact—so I had no compunction about enjoying a few drinks before walking back home in the early hours. However, as a result I need to stroll back there and pick up my car—and I thought I'd take in a slap-up breakfast and a swim while I'm there. I merely wondered whether you'd like to join me. It's a beautiful pool—and they have a first-rate chef.'

'Why on earth should I want to do that?' she bit out, screwing her eyes tight shut against the image of his body slicing through the silky blue water of a swimming-pool. She'd seen enough of him this morning to last her a lifetime.

'Suit yourself,' he said breezily, and she heard the slap of his feet on the cold floor and the creak of the hinges as he made to close the door. Then he hesitated for a moment. 'Remember what I said about trespassing, now won't you, Livvy?' he rejoined, and she could hear the amusement in his voice.

'The whole notion of trespassing is puerile and pathetic,' she muttered, her eyes glued to the fire. 'It's just a childish game designed to annoy me.'

'Mmm,' Leon said speculatively. 'That's what I decided last night when I was walking back here under the stars, but I changed my mind when I saw you crouched over that little fire. Now I think it's an excellent idea.'

'Do you? Why?'

'Because you look gorgeous crouching down like that in those tight jeans.'

'That's a disgusting thing to say——'

'Oh, get off your high horse, Livvy, and learn to take a compliment,' he growled with exasperation. 'My reasoning has nothing to do with your jeans as it happens, and everything to do with your wonderful principles. You see, I keep thinking of that story of yours... Old what's-her-name, your heroine, she's crippled, isn't she? Do you think she'd be able to kneel down like that to blow on the fire? There were no modern conveniences in her day, after all, and without a fire her very life could be in jeopardy, stuck in some peasant's hovel as she was. I just don't see how she could fail to find her suitor's affluence tempting, do you? At any rate, I'm sure you'll agree that by insisting that you keep to your eighteenth-century kitchen I'm actually assisting you in your research. What do you think?'

But he didn't wait for a reply. And anyway, Livvy had no breath to waste on speech as she puffed frantically on the last, fading flame.

When he returned she was in her gloomy sitting-room, examining some of her work. She heard first the car and then his footsteps and rushed out to catch him. She found him in the hall, standing in front of his office desk, leaning forward, his weight taken on the knuckles of one hand and a telephone receiver in the other. The sight of him made anger jump inside her as wildly as a fish flinging itself upstream. He was so outrageously attractive. It threw her off balance. It wasn't fair.

Swallowing her anger as best she could, she burst out, 'Leon! At last! Look, last night you forgot to say that I could use the library as well as the other rooms you gave me. The thing is, it's obvious that I must be allowed to go in there because it's part of the deal. But rather than risk being accused of *trespassing* again I've been waiting until you got back——'

'Hello? Rafe...? Yeah, Leon... Terrific... Uh-huh... I got the message all right but I couldn't get back to you yesterday morning. Anyhow, I just thought I'd confirm the arrangement. Good. Yes. Fine. I'll see you then, OK?'

He replaced the receiver very deliberately, then slowly straightened up and swung around to face her. 'What was that you were saying?'

'I just wanted to get your permission to use the library today,' she muttered, glowering at him.

He smiled slowly, his blue eyes cool. 'No.'

'Now look here, Leon, that's just not on. One of the items on the balance sheet which was supposed to accrue to me was the use of the library to search for my document. And although I've been trying to avoid warfare, if you stick to your guns over that one then battle will have to commence.'

'You mean you'll give me the opportunity to wrest you forcibly from the library?' He pursed his lips and narrowed his eyes. 'Livvy,' he growled warningly, 'don't tempt me...'

'Oh, for goodness' sake!'

'Goodness will have nothing to do with it, I can assure you...' he muttered, his blue eyes glittering.

Livvy swallowed. 'Now look here. The thing is——'

'The thing is,' he broke in scornfully, 'that you can't use the library today because you're coming away with me. When we get back, *then* you can use the library.'

'I... What?'

'I thought we'd take a honeymoon.'

Livvy stared at him, her mouth open. 'What?'

'Oh, there's no need to gawp like that. I shan't try to *kiss* you if that's what's bothering you. You can definitely trust me. That's a promise.'

Ignoring the sinking feeling in the pit of her stomach, she said haughtily, 'Well, in that case why on earth do you want to take me away on honeymoon?'

'Firstly, although you can trust me, I don't yet feel that I can trust you. If I left you here you'd go and cook yourself lunch in my kitchen, wouldn't you?'

'Why should you care?' she countered, hoping that she wasn't blushing a guilty blush.

'I wasn't the one who cared about sharing a kitchen in the first place. You were. I'm simply trying to help you live up to your high ideals, Olivia.'

Livvy remembered the tandoori chicken and blushed so definitively that she could feel her skin burning. 'I only wanted a *cupboard* to myself, not a whole kitchen,' she grumbled.

'But, Livvy, that kitchen of yours is wonderful,' he drawled sarcastically. 'You were so dismayed when you thought I'd had it ripped out . . . What was it you said?'

'Well, it's true that I thought it should be preserved, but that didn't mean that I thought there ought not be any alternative facilities. You know. More modern ones.'

'Like the ones that have been installed in the Edwardian wash-house? Namely my nice, convenient, modern kitchen?'

She nodded dismally. 'Well, I suppose so. But not quite so impossibly out of character with the house.'

'Does that mean you actually want to share a kitchen with me now?' he asked contemptuously.

'No. Definitely not.'

'Good. Because I wasn't about to suggest it. Now go and have a wash, there's a dear. You have a smut on your cheek. You can't go on honeymoon with a dirty face.'

'I'm not honeymooning with you and that's final.'

'Oh, yes, you are. The other reason which I have not yet got around to mentioning is that I think it would lend our marriage a certain amount of credibility.'

'Oh, but really! If you'd wanted a fake honeymoon as well as a fake marriage you should have said so from the outset! Anyhow, I can't see how this marriage is going to have any credibility at all if you keep on seeing other women!'

'Other women?' he hooted incredulously. 'Good God, I wouldn't have the strength! One is more than enough.'

'Ha! What about Katya, eh? Just exactly who is Katya?'

'She's my sister, Livvy,' he groaned wearily. 'I wondered when you were going to ask about Katya. She's my sister.'

'Pigs might fly...' Livvy muttered derisively.

His face blazed with delighted mirth. 'Are you jealous, Livvy?'

'Jealous?' And she arched her eyebrows sarcastically. 'Now why should I be jealous of your *sister*?'

He shrugged, clearly still amused. 'OK. Have it your own way,' he returned mildly.

'Thank you,' she returned. 'In that case I'm off to use the library.'

'No, you're not. You're off to wash your face.' He glanced at his watch. 'And hurry up; we're short of time.'

Livvy puffed out a huge sigh and stared sulkily at her trainers. 'I *can't* wash,' she complained. 'There's still no water in my basin. Can I use your bathroom?'

Leon narrowed his eyes and shook his head. 'I should hate to be the instrument of your downfall,' he said seriously. 'You'll just have to use the outside pump in the yard as Rosamund would have done before her marriage. The plumbing in this house is extraordinary, isn't it? All those water closets keep diverting the supply to fuel their own cisterns, you see. It'll be much better once the builders have ripped everything out. Don't worry. They'll soon be here with their crowbars and jemmies and lump hammers, stripping out all the old panelling and ripping out all the old pipes and hacking off all the old plaster!'

'Vandal!' she muttered.

'You mean that you're in favour of the WCs staying put after all?'

'No,' she conceded wearily. But the mention of the builders was ringing bells inside her head. 'Not them. But I am in favour of anything that is done to the house being done sympathetically and with respect for the building's heritage,' she added primly. 'So it's just as well that the house is now half mine, isn't it? You can't stop me from using the library after all,' she concluded triumphantly.

He tilted his head to one side and smiled. 'Technically you're right, of course,' and then he sauntered across to her and caught hold of one of her hands. She froze, leaving her fingers limply in his grasp and struggling to master the melting weakness which assailed her the moment his flesh touched hers. He flexed one arm theatrically and then lifted her hand and pressed her fingertips to his bicep, iron-hard beneath the rough cotton of his shirt. She flinched, then dragged her hand away.

'What's the matter? I thought you were only interested in me for my muscles?' he mocked.

'I'm interested in them from a visual point of view only. I'm certainly not interested in their tactile qualities,' she said huskily. She cleared her throat. 'Anyway, you didn't do that in order to help me with my anatomy studies. You did it to demonstrate your superior physical strength.'

But Leon just stared at her impassively. Then he said, 'Fifteen minutes, OK? Clean face, bag packed for an overnight stay. I'll see you back here in the hall.'

And then he walked away.

'Stop!' she called angrily in his wake. 'I'm not coming!'

'You are,' he sighed, continuing to move forward. 'The nature of the deal dictates that we do nothing to draw attention to the fact that we're not married in the full sense of the word. It was implicit in the agreement.'

'And Katya?' she spat back. 'What about Katya? Was she implicit in the agreement too? Oh, and please don't try insisting that she's your sister because, apart from the fact that she doesn't sound like the sort of sister who'd miss her brother's wedding if she had anything to do with it, she rang me this morning and virtually told me that she *wasn't*!'

He turned to look at her, frowning. 'Which phone did you take the call on?' he asked.

'The one in the kitchen.'

He stiffened quite visibly, and turned more than his hair in order to survey her with icy disdain. 'My kitchen, I presume? The one you're not supposed to be using?'

'Er...yes.'

'Warfare. Go and get that bag packed, Livvy, before I force you to.'

Defeated, she stumped off towards the staircase.

They travelled in his car. She had removed the smut but her hair reeked of woodsmoke, as did her skin.

'Are we going to a hotel?' she asked longingly, picturing gallons of steaming water.

'A castle. A half-ruined castle.'

'Where?'

'Wales. Overlooking the sea.'

'Oh. I see. What a romantic location!'

'You don't see,' he replied, and then he added, 'Yet.'

'And just what is that supposed to mean?'

In response Leon switched on the radio and listened to the cricket.

His car made marvellous time on the motorway without his needing to drive at all recklessly. As they bypassed Cardiff she glanced at the clock on the dashboard. Twenty to twelve. 'Lunchtime,' she said hopefully.

He didn't reply.

'We don't want to leave it too late if we're going to stop,' she said. 'Everywhere gets so crowded . . .'

'You're right. We won't bother. I hate crowds.'

Livvy closed her eyes and listened to her stomach rumbling against the background hum of cricket commentary and car engines and said nothing more.

Gloomily she peered through the tinted glass at Wales flashing past her until they came off the motorway and began skirting Swansea. 'Are we nearly there?' she asked.

'Not far. The castle is out on the Gower peninsula, on a cliff overlooking the sea.'

'Then wouldn't Swansea be a good place to have lunch?'

He smiled. 'It would. But I'm afraid I couldn't manage another morsel after that magnificent breakfast I had.'

CHAPTER EIGHT

THE castle was not what Livvy had expected. For a start it wasn't a real castle, but a rambling collection of buildings, the most imposing of which was a nineteenth-century house built of grey stone and, as Livvy's mother would have said, 'got up to look like a castle'. It was also a youth hostel.

'What are we doing here?' Livvy asked uneasily, glancing back at his car. Youth hostels provided cheap, basic lodgings for people on walking holidays, didn't they? The filthy rich in their fast cars usually avoided them like the plague.

'It's for sale,' Leon said, looking up at the façade.

'Are you going to buy it?'

'That depends.'

She eyes him suspiciously. 'Are you planning to modernise it too?'

'Yep.'

She patted one of the mellow grey stones. 'Poor castle,' she murmured. 'Well, what are we doing just standing here? Are we waiting for the estate agent to arrive to show us round?'

'Not as such, but I *have* made arrangements to spend the rest of the day examining the place. I'm meeting a few other people who are involved in other aspects of the survey in an hour or so. It'll take us quite a while to assess it.'

'You got me here under false pretences,' she observed. 'You said this was a honeymoon.'

'*Livvy . . .*' he reproved drily. 'Don't tell me now that you wish we'd made use of the facilities at the Golden Nightingale?'

'Of course not. But the thing is, if you're going to spend the afternoon surveying a building, why do you need me here?'

'Because it would have looked strange to have left you behind,' he returned evenly. 'We've only been married for twenty-four hours—though I have to admit it already feels more like twenty-four years. Oh, and in case you're worried that people will consider us too unconventional, I might as well tell you that I'll be taking you to the Solomon Islands for a more socially acceptable honeymoon in September whether you like it or not— so don't start one of your infernal arguments on the subject. At any rate, this particular job couldn't be postponed. I heard yesterday that a rival firm has put in a bid.'

She laid her cheek against the wall. 'Trashing buildings . . .' she sighed. 'It's obviously very important work. So what shall I do with myself this afternoon? Follow you round making cow eyes?'

He pointed around the side of the building towards the sea. 'There's a path there leading to a beach. You can spend the afternoon sunning yourself and swimming.'

She looked up at the sky. 'What if the weather changes? There are some clouds blowing over.'

'Then you can sit in my car,' he said irritably, following it up with one of his lazy, dazzling smiles. 'I'd like that.'

Livvy's heart lurched. 'Would you? Why?'

'Because you could keep track of the cricket score for me.'

Smarting inwardly, she said blithely, 'Actually, I'll enjoy a ramble. I'm fond of the great outdoors. And if it rains... well, I expect I'll survive.'

'Mmm...' He was looking up at the roof now, frowning, his hands on his hips and appearing to concentrate very hard. 'Your heroine would have survived being perpetually damp, after all,' he continued slyly, keeping his eyes on the roof. 'The houses didn't have damp-proof courses in those days and mackintoshes hadn't been invented. I expect the average British peasant was practically mouldy with damp most of the year round.'

Livvy bit her lip hard, battling not just with her annoyance but with voracious hunger pangs as well. 'What about food?' she asked sweetly. 'Have you any plans?'

'We'll eat in the village pub this evening, I expect. All the members of the survey team will want a chance to compare notes, anyway, so it'll be a good opportunity...'

'Nothing until then?' she queried sweetly.

He took his eyes off the roof then and regarded her impassively. 'Hungry? Oh, dear.' His tongue appeared in his cheek. 'Never mind, Livvy. Good for your research, after all. Peasants often went hungry.'

'Where are we staying?'

'Oh, at the same pub. It offers bed and breakfast.'

'But we're not far from civilisation,' she frowned, picturing a pub bedroom with a double bed taking up most of the space. 'Isn't there a big hotel near by which would be more comfortable?' A hotel with suites of rooms in which two people could easily lose themselves...

'Livvy!' he exclaimed, feigning horror. 'Don't tell me that one glimpse of the Golden Nightingale has won you over? Or were you a closet materialist all along? You'll be telling me you're a shopaholic next!'

'Oh, really!'

'Do you think Rosamund would have turned her nose up at the village inn the night after she got married?'

'What are you trying to prove, Leon?' she muttered.

'My point,' came his laconic reply.

Livvy swivelled on her heel and went back to the car. She was damned if she'd let him know how furious she was. He'd blame it all on her hunger and construe it as irrefutable proof that her story was trash. But darn it, why was he so determined to prove that Rosamund hadn't been pure in heart—that she'd been tempted by her suitor's wealth? Well, she'd show him that women, no matter what century they inhabited, could fend for themselves without relying on a man for anything! She wasn't quite sure how it would help Gallagher's doomed employees, but it was a point worth making none the less. To that end she pulled angrily at the car door, but it wouldn't open.

'Leon!' she called peremptorily. 'The car is locked. I need to get my bag if I'm to go to the beach.'

He kept his eyes locked on the building, but put one hand in his trouser pocket and withdrew a black plastic device which he pointed at the car. The sound of an electronic bleep was followed by a muffled click, and when she next tried the door it opened without difficulty.

Grabbing her bag, she made off in the direction Leon had indicated. He was squatting on his hunkers, close against the wall, examining the stones by then. She glowered at the broad expanse of his shoulders, delectably outlined beneath his blue chambray shirt, then fled before he caught her at it and accused her of ogling. Huh! She might have ogled him the first time she saw him, but she hadn't known the man then!

The winding path arrived, eventually, at a golden beach strewn with sunbathers.

'Is there a café or shop anywhere near?' she asked a somnolent middle-aged woman.

'About three miles, at the far end of the next bay...' came the reply.

Three and three-quarter miles later Livvy staggered up to a tea hut and ordered two coffees and two cheese and pickle rolls and two chocolate biscuits.

'Left you to do all the carrying, has he?' grinned the woman behind the counter as she juggled with her purchases.

Livvy nodded wearily, balancing one polystyrene cup with a plastic lid on top of the other. It was a beautiful beach. What a shame she was in too foul a mood to enjoy it. And what a shame it was beginning to spot with rain.

When she got back it was to find six or seven assorted vehicles parked around Leon's like a fan club. She wandered around the extraordinary building until she came upon the owners of the vehicles, standing in a group in the sunshine—the weather had turned nice again— and looking very congenial. Leon stood out from the crowd, with his superior height and strong colouring and astonishing good looks. He said something to the assembled crowd and then put his hand affectionately on the shoulder of an attractive woman with short blonde hair, and everybody laughed.

Livvy ran her fingers impatiently through her own damp, tangled hair. She felt profoundly reluctant to encounter Leon while he was with all those people. It was obvious she was the only one to have been caught outdoors in the cloudburst and she looked a mess. She was considering slinking off again when he spied her. He took his hand from the shoulder of the blonde woman and extended it welcomingly towards her. 'Come over here, Livvy,' he called, his face and voice smiling. But his eyes, even from a distance, chilled her blood. 'Everybody's looking forward to meeting you,' he added.

Livvy plastered a rigid smile to her face. Meekly she made her way across to him, hanging on to her composure for grim death as he pulled her towards him and wrapped his arms around her shoulders. Her heart was drumming and her mouth felt dry. 'Olivia...you're wet!' he exclaimed silkily. 'Did you get caught in that awful downpour? Oh, you poor, poor thing. You'll end up with a dreadful chill,' and his fingers tinkered indiscreetly with the skin at the nape of her neck under the cover of her hair, until she feared she might scream.

'I'm fine,' she protested, trying to steady her voice so that it wouldn't betray her rampant lust. 'Good grief, Leon—I can survive a drenching, surely? Think of all those generations of people who survived before they even invented the mackintosh, for goodness' sake!'

But he shook his head and hugged her close, bringing her out in goose-bumps. She felt the hardness of her nipples rubbing through the layers of clothing at his muscular chest.

'But your clothes are positively wringing wet!' he murmured, and the one hand which wasn't clamping her against him smoothed the sleeve of her clinging silk blouse up and down over her upper arm.

Livvy turned her head away from him so that she was no longer forced to inhale the warmth of his flesh overhung by the woody aroma of his cologne, but she could still feel the hardness of his body pressed against the length of hers, and the sensation was every bit as overpowering as the scent of his skin had been. Inside she was turning to fire. None the less, she managed to keep her plastic grin going and turned her big green eyes appealingly at the assembled crowd, all of whom seemed to be eyeing her with an indulgence more normally ac-

corded to children. 'Honestly!' she exclaimed humor-
ously. 'I'll soon dry out. It's no problem.'

Unfortunately she seemed to have caught the eye of
a bearded man in late middle age, clad in the sort of
thorn-proof tweeds she associated with the gentry
of yester-year. 'Damp?' he said grimly in the plummiest
of plummy voices. 'Consumption, my dear. People used
to go down with it like ninepins in the days before mackintoshes. The white plague, it was called. Dampness was
a scourge. Can't be too careful, even in this day and
age.'

Livvy frowned. 'Look, I'm a perfectly healthy young
woman, and the sun's back out again now. I'll dry off
in no time at all.'

But Leon was shaking his head. 'Rafe's right,' he said
firmly. 'I'm going to take you down to the village to
warm up. You can take a nice hot bath and change into
fresh clothes. I'm sure everyone will excuse me if I disappear for half an hour?'

There was a murmur of assent and several exchanges
of knowing looks. Livvy winced. Ah... the young bride
and the besotted bridegroom... No wonder nobody had
backed her up when she'd challenged Leon's absurd
concern. They were all assuming that the pair of love-
birds were merely looking for an excuse to be alone
together, and Rafe no doubt believed he had done her
a favour. With a sigh she tugged away from her treacherous husband and made for the car. It was by chance
that she noticed Leon catch the eye of the blonde woman
as he followed her. 'Catch up with you later, Sonia,' he
murmured. 'OK?'

Once settled in the car she buckled herself in and kept
her eyes fixed on the windscreen. 'What was that all
about?' she ground out.

'I felt sorry for you when I saw you looking so bedraggled,' he said tersely. 'I thought I'd give you an excuse to return to civilisation. There'll be plenty of food and hot water at the pub. You can have a break from being a peasant girl for a while and I can sit in the car and catch up on the test match while I wait.'

She glared at the tinted glass. 'I don't need a break from anything except you. There's no need to wait for me. Go back to your...your castle straight away.'

His mouth made itself into a straight, thin line. 'Dammit, I *didn't* feel sorry for you at all, as it happens, and I still don't,' he muttered savagely. 'I had to get away from that crew because holding you like that was doing things to me which are better done in private.'

'Am I supposed to swoon with delight at that admission?' she snapped, recalling only too vividly the glance he had slanted at Sonia.

He turned his head and looked frostily at her. 'No. Anything I felt was just an automatic reaction to *your* response to me,' he said unkindly. 'In that wet silk blouse it was more than obvious how you were feeling.'

'I was chilled. That's all it was,' she said archly. 'So what do you plan to do now? Drive me somewhere quiet for a half an hour's *privacy*?'

'Oh, no,' he returned acidly. 'I don't relish the idea of acting on my instinctive drives with someone who isn't even prepared to admit that she has any.'

'Oh, I have *drives*,' she huffed out bitterly. 'It's just that you do nothing for them at all.'

There was a silence during which she sensed that Leon was glowering at her. Then he snapped, 'This is nonsense. You were as turned on as I was. But as neither of us gives a damn about how the other feels I'll take you to the pub. You can do what you like once you get there.'

When they arrived in the courtyard of the pretty inn Leon took her overnight bag and walked ahead of her to check in.

The room was just as she had imagined it. It had its own small bathroom. 'Are you sleeping in the bath?' she asked nervously.

'No chance.'

'Then why did you book in here? Couldn't you have arranged for us to have separate rooms somehow?'

'No.'

'Then why?' she insisted, her cheeks flaming.

'Because it seemed pointless booking a separate room for myself when I shan't be sleeping in it.'

'Oh...?' Livvy cleared her throat. 'And exactly where will you be?'

'With Sonia. Working. Good grief, when I acquired a wife I didn't imagine I'd get nagged to death within twenty-four hours!'

Working? All night? In a pub in the Welsh countryside? Livvy almost snorted out loud. 'Sexist rat,' she muttered furiously.

'Oh, shut up, Olivia. I didn't mean that wives in general nag. Simply that you do.'

'Nag? I merely enquired as to where you'd be spending the night. Surely that doesn't count as nagging?'

'And I merely told you that I'd be spending the night with Sonia and that it was none of your business.'

'It may not be my business, but I'm sure Katya would consider it hers. She seemed very concerned to know where you spent last night, after all.'

At which Leon glared at her for a very long time, his eyes practically scalding her skin. Eventually he said, 'And are you planning to make it your business to tell her?'

Livvy shrugged. 'No. You are free to live your life any way you choose, Leon Roche. I may have principles that aren't business principles, but at least I don't go around making other people's lives a misery.'

He shrugged, put her small holdall on the bed, and then with a fluid, easy movement leant across and took her shoulder-bag from her. While she looked on, poker-faced and baffled, he opened it and took out her purse. He stuffed it in the pocket of his jeans. 'I'll see you downstairs about seven . . . seven-thirty.'

'No chance,' she flared back. Honestly, how dared he expect her to fall in with his unscrupulous wiles? It was one thing behaving like a wife in front of a group of anonymous business colleagues, quite another doing it under the eye of the woman with whom he was planning to spend the night, and who would obviously know otherwise.

'But Livvy, you must eat.'

'Overall, I agree. But not in your company. Anyway, I'm sure Rosamund occasionally went hungry. It's no big deal.'

'But you've scarcely had a thing all day.'

'I have. I ate on the beach. And before you accuse me of being unprincipled, let me point out that they had convenience food in the eighteenth century as well.'

'Wow! I didn't realise McDonald's went back that far.'

Livvy hissed with annoyance. 'Hot-chestnut men. Muffin men. Things like that. And there was something called flummery which people used to buy at fairs and so on. It was made from sweetened oatmeal and milk and it was delicious.'

Leon's eyebrows arched. 'Good grief, Livvy, I knew that rural Wales was a little behind the times, but don't tell me they were serving flummery on the beach?'

She gave him a very baleful look. 'The point is that I can fend for myself. Now give me back my purse.'

'No.'

'Why have you taken it?'

'I'm removing your rotor arm.'

'What?'

'It's what you do to a car to immobilise it. Without money you can't do a bunk.'

She glared at him, and then snatched her bag back from him and rummaged through the contents. Finally she found a plastic card and held it out to him. 'In that case you'd better take this as well.'

He frowned. 'It's a telephone card. For using payphones.'

'That's right. If I'd made it back to civilisation I might have telephoned Katya and told her what you were up to, mightn't I?' she snapped. 'But with the card I could still telephone her from here despite having no money. I do have principles and I *am* trustworthy, believe it or not. Now clear off and don't come back until you're ready to drive me back to Bristol.'

'You live in Hereford now,' he said mildly, opening the door.

'Wrong!' she exclaimed. 'Bristol. I shall see a solicitor as soon as I can and arrange a formal separation.'

And then Leon, who already had his back to her, began to laugh that round, rich laugh of his, closed the door and walked away.

Livvy forced herself to wash in cold water—warm would have been cheating—and ate three little packets of sugar that had found their way into her bag from cafeteria tables. She kept the worst of the hunger at bay by drinking water, which was all right except that it meant she kept waking in the night to go to the loo. Around two she heard convivial laughter on the landing outside and the plummiest of plummy voices wishing everybody goodnight.

When next she awoke it was seven-thirty and Leon was in the room. 'Oh, it's you,' she said bitterly, peeping out from over the bedclothes.

But he didn't reply.

She stuck her nose out over the top of the sheet. He was unbuttoning his shirt, his back to her. Infuriatingly her eyes refused to close. He took off his shirt ... all that acreage of silken skin, golden-brown, stretched tautly across his muscular frame ... She gulped and pulled the sheet up to hide her face.

'Awake, Livvy?' he asked.

'You're not supposed to speak before breakfast,' she mumbled from under the bedclothes.

'I've had breakfast already. Grapefruit, cereal, egg and bacon and sausage and tomatoes and toast and marmalade. And butter, lots of butter. And a big pot of piping hot coffee with warm milk. I don't know how I managed to eat so much after that enormous steak I put away last night. Not to mention the gateau ...'

Livvy groaned.

'Hurry up and go downstairs and you can have as much as you like ...'

'I'm fine,' she protested weakly.

'You'll faint.'

'I won't. Anyway, what are you doing stripping off in here if you're not getting ready for breakfast?'

'I'm going to use the bathroom. Unless you want to use it first?'

'I can use the basin in the corner over there. Washing in cold water is no problem, but I think a cold bath might be carrying it a bit far.'

Leon groaned. 'Oh, come on, Livvy, enough is enough. You can wash and eat, you know. I simply hoped that a little material deprivation would help you see your heroine's point of view more clearly. You don't have to kill yourself in the process.'

'I'm not killing myself! I'm all right.'

'OK. But you're being childish. Surely you've had enough of a taste of the hard life to see my point?'

Angry, Livvy stuck her hot red face above the covers and scowled at him. The sight which met her eyes almost made her yelp. He was facing her, wearing nothing but his jeans, and he was smoothing the hairs on his stomach very slowly with the tips of his fingers. He badly needed a shave.

'Look, you started this, not me! You think I should just cave in and...' She sucked in a huge breath. Thank goodness she'd been red-faced even before she'd come up for air... 'And just accept that Rosamund was so wishy-washy that one whiff of roast pheasant and figgy pudding would have destroyed all her values at a stroke! Well, my point will take a lot longer than thirty-six hours to prove, but I'll prove it in the end! Six months from now you'll be laughing the other side of your face, Leon Roche. I'll admit that it'll take me a while to acclimatise because I'm not used to deprivation in the way that she would have been, but I can assure you that I can last six months without modern conveniences without any trouble at all.'

He shrugged, one eyebrow up and the other down, his blue eyes freezingly cold. She ran her tongue over her dry lips. It was astonishing how many muscles were involved in a single shrug. The pectoral muscles, for a start, firmed quite conspicuously, and the biceps swelled, and the collarbones rippled in and out of sight and...

'Perhaps you'd like to dig yourself an earth closet when we get back, then...' he murmured.

Livvy's green eyes widened, and her full lips compressed into a bitter line. 'Oh, shut up!' She dived back under the sheet.

'I take it that means no? Jolly good. I shall be about forty minutes in the bathroom—taking a lovely, long, hot bath. Perhaps you could make sure you're packed and ready to go by then?'

Forty minutes later, Leon, looking absolutely marvellous in a grey and white striped shirt and forest-green trousers, his crisp curls glossy, his expression speaking of well-fed contentment, loaded the bags into the car while Livvy slouched, pale and ravenous, her auburn waves looking a little ragged after the previous day's drenching, in the passenger seat. An early morning haze hung over the sun-filled landscape. In the distance could be glimpsed the silver sea.

Sonia appeared, looking every bit as replete as Leon, and sauntered towards him smiling sunnily. 'Bye, Leon...'

He dazzled her with his smile. 'I'll catch up with you in town, Son.'

'Mmm. Thanks for last night.'

'It was a pleasure.'

'It *was* good, wasn't it?'

'Fantastic. A once-in-a-lifetime experience—except that now I know how good it can be I intend repeating it.' He looked right into her eyes then, keeping the indolent, brilliant smile going, and wagged his finger at her. 'Now remember what I said...'

'Leon, I explained——'

But he put the tip of one finger on her lips to silence her. 'I want *you*,' he said emphatically.

Sonia laughed. 'And you always get what you want? Is that it?'

'Yes,' he returned, dropping his hands but maintaining the eye contact.

'But——'

'You and only you,' he repeated determinedly, keeping his eyes locked on to hers as he got into the car.

Sonia smiled and wrinkled up her nose and blew him a kiss. Leon started the engine and waved. Sonia gave a huge wave. Livvy gave a cross, regal little wave and thanked heaven that she'd had no breakfast. All of this was making her feel quite sick.

'She's a great woman, is Sonia,' said Leon conversationally as they bowled down the country road.

'Single and willing,' said Livvy sharply. 'You could have asked *her* to marry you.'

'She's not single as it happens,' returned Leon equably.

Livvy snorted loudly. Did the man have no principles at all? Not to mention Sonia herself!

'Did you enjoy your breakfast, Livvy?'

'I didn't have breakfast.'

He groaned. 'Honestly? You mean you haven't eaten a thing? Not even a slice of toast?'

'No.'

'But Rafe was expecting you to join him. He's a social historian. He wanted to give you some tips.'

'Well, do apologise to him next time you see him,' she snapped. Honestly... Was she expected to believe that Leon would employ a social historian to do a structural survey? He'd say anything to prove his point...

But Leon said nothing more. All the way back home.

Once they were across the threshold Livvy went straight to the library to stake out her territory. Leon disappeared into his kitchen to make himself a snack.

The smell of toast seemed to permeate every corner of the house. Unable to bear it any longer, Livvy went to her room, changed into a baggy T-shirt and a pair of leggings and took off in her car to Hereford. She came back a couple of hours later, munching a chocolate bar and with plenty of the sort of food that would keep without a fridge and which required no cooking. She had also bought an electric kettle for her sitting-room.

She dumped the shopping in her kitchen then returned to the library and surveyed the shelves. She had already walked around the room once, letting her eyes do the searching, but to no avail. Clearly she was going to have to open the glass-fronted cases and begin searching for real. But the glass-fronted cases were locked. Irritably she went back to her sitting-room, took out a sharp pencil and began outlining one of the illuminated capitals which would open every page of text. But the room was so gloomy that despite sitting next to the window and screwing up her eyes it proved impossible to work.

Right, then. She'd just have to go and tell Leon that the room wouldn't do. She couldn't possibly work in there and that was that. She went into the hall and shouted his name out loud. There was no reply. She opened the front door to check that his car was there, and it was. Then she went and knocked on the door of his kitchen and his bedroom and walked right into the enormous drawing-room which she had seen him use. He wasn't there either. In fact, the house was full of the sort of echoy silence that suggested she was in it all on her own.

She tried a few more doors, searching for a suitably light room, but a surprising number of them proved to be locked. Except the water closets. Finally she returned to his drawing-room, which was undoubtedly the lightest room in the house. Nervously she glanced around, wondering how he would react when he discovered that she was using his space as a studio. Not well, she concluded airily. And then she walked over to look out of

the window behind the couch and realised that it wasn't
a window at all but the glass door to a conservatory.
Ideal! What could be lighter?

It took all her strength to shove the enormous, dusty
Victorian couch away from the door, but she was pleased
that she'd made the effort. The conservatory proved to
be huge—a wonderful concoction of wrought iron and
glass, dating from the last century as far as she could
tell, and quite dry. There was even a table and a couple
of battered wicker chairs in there. She fetched her
drawing things, set the paper on the table and stood over
it, forcing herself to concentrate very, very hard on the
fine details. Excellent. Work was the perfect antidote to
Leon Roche. What a rat that man was...

She must have been there for a half an hour, and was
carefully inking in the outline of the letter, when she
heard a creak. Her blood stood still in her veins and
every hair on her body stood on end. What was it? She
held her breath and strained her ears. She could hear
the faint pad of feet on the tiled floor and could feel the
air move almost menacingly. *Someone was creeping up
behind her.* She could even sense the imperceptible
soughing of breath behind her head. Her heart started
to race but her limbs were frozen with fear.

And then a large, male hand clamped itself hard over
her mouth and a fearsomely strong male arm pinned
itself around her like a vice, and, kicking and threshing
with panic, she was lifted clear of the floor. It was Leon.
She could taste him and smell him, and the juddering
glimpses of wrist and hand which met her blurred vision
as she struggled helplessly, trying to force a scream past
her gagged lips, were so unmistakable that there could
be no doubt. She was moving backwards through the
air, being carried purposefully through the door, her legs
kicking out with a violence she hadn't known she pos-

sessed, and then, horrifyingly, his hands freed her mouth only to snatch at her shoulder and lift her even higher, hurling her hard over the couch so that she bounced on its ancient springs. In the moment that his hands left her body she tried to roll away, but in an instant he was upon her, diving over the back of the couch with a frightening intensity, his eyes, as she glimpsed them, alight with rage. She struggled beneath the weight of him, succeeding only in tumbling them both on to the floor. Again he grabbed her, his grip like iron, and again his hand flew to her face to gag her mouth. But before he achieved his target she opened her mouth wide and let out a piercing scream.

The air seemed to shiver with it. Round and round echoed the sound in the big, musty room. And then something inhuman groaned in reply, curdling Livvy's blood. Her stomach clenched with fright. Her throat tightened. With the most fearful clashing and crashing and splintering, half the conservatory fell in.

Appalled, Livvy lay on the carpet, pinned in place by Leon's uncompromisingly masculine form, transfixed by the sound of thin Victorian glass dropping like daggers on to the tiled floor where she had stood just moments before. Her heart bounced in her chest. Through the layers of clothing she could feel Leon's own heart pounding steadily, could feel his big ribcage swelling and collapsing as he dragged in hungry breaths. She began to shake, her teeth chattering with horror, funny little sounds choking out of her throat. She was cold to the marrow, her pale cheeks wintry, while frantic, blurry little screams shrieked in her head.

As the great din of destruction echoed at last into silence, Leon eased himself off her. Freed from the weight of his torso and thighs, she felt numbingly vulnerable and exposed.

For a moment she lay huddled and still, very alone. Then, awash with fear, she clawed her way across the worn Persian carpet back towards the source of all her security. He was lying flat on his back, a few feet away from her, one leg crooked and his hand over his eyes, inhaling and exhaling heavily through his parted lips. Her fingers dug into his midriff like claws. 'Leon?' she whimpered.

With a loud groan he rolled back against her, his arms sweeping out to encompass her, his thigh crossing her hips and covering her like a blanket. Shuddering, she curled into his arms like a kitten, tucking her head under his chin, slipping her hands under his arms and around him and pressing her ear close to his chest where she could hear the drumming of his heart.

CHAPTER NINE

HUDDLED against him, Livvy plucked at Leon's shirt with shivering fingers, easing open the buttons, searching for his skin. Beyond the cloth she would find the heat of his flesh...the living warmth of the man against which she was driven to chafe her chilled bones. And indeed, no sooner had her hands slipped between the edges of the cool fabric and laid themselves tremblingly on the soft, springy curls of his heaving chest than her own flesh burned hot. She nipped at his shoulder with her chattering teeth, feeling a fire course through her so fast that she gasped aloud.

'Livvy?' he said thickly.

'P-please...' she stammered. 'Oh, please...'

His face, already buried in her hair, began to mouthe kisses against her scalp then. His barbed chin rubbed urgently against her forehead, scorching her skin. Hungrily she turned her face upwards, her round eyes begging him for...for what? Her body clenched against his, giving the response that her throat was too parched to voice. There was a pregnant moment of stillness, and then his arms came around her in a bear hug. His mouth dragged down over her eyes and her high cheekbones, his teeth smooth against her skin until his hard mouth found her soft, quivering lips and buried them in the fiercest of kisses. Desperately her tongue darted into the safe haven of his mouth, testing every moist surface with its tip, revelling in the taste of him.

Livvy was lost. Deeper and deeper she sank into the whirlpool of arousal, spurred by his hard, male body

grinding urgently against her pliant flesh. Her hands
moved inside his shirt, tugging it free until she had her
palms flat upon his shoulders, stroking and then clawing
at that silken skin which had, until now, tantalised only
her eyes. Her fingertips found the indentation of his spine
and traced it lower, so that he shuddered in her arms,
the solid muscles of his back hardening like iron under
her touch.

Then his entire body tautened. His thighs straddled
hers, his knees dug into the floor and he rose above her,
tearing his mouth from hers before planting his hard lips
almost savagely against one burgeoning nipple, peaking
through the soft cotton of her T-shirt. His teeth nipped
gently at its roundness time and again until she cried out
with delight and then he began to suck hard both on
cotton and flesh, his other hand taunting her other breast
with small circular movements.

Her breathing was ragged, her throat full of pleading
cries, and her whole body so sensitised that it actually
seemed to be swollen with desire. When he finally pushed
her clothing roughly upwards so that her breasts could
taste the warm moistness of his mouth, something deep
inside her scorched with desire. And when his tongue
touched her nipples they thrust demandingly against his
mouth, hungry only for him.

Further and further he carried her, arousing her to the
point where she found herself beyond control, dragging
at the waistband of his trousers, her hips arching to meet
his in an instinctive invitation. At some point he paused
long enough to tear her leggings from her and drag her
T-shirt over her head. She was shocked and excited at
the sight of him then, a high colour burning beneath his
olive skin, the blue of his eyes misted, his pupils dilated,
his lips parted. His face was at once familiar and yet
profoundly altered. My lover's face, she found herself

thinking, and she seemed to see stardust on the bruised swell of his lower lip and gold upon his brow. A great swell of emotion squeezed her heart, bringing bright foolish tears to her eyes.

And then he tore off his own shirt, pushed down his trousers and was on top of her, every male inch of him crushed against her. Eagerly she opened to him. Urgently, powerfully, he entered her. There was a silence for a moment, as if the world had halted on its axis, and then he was thrusting savagely, and so shockingly rigid in her arms that she was nearly afraid, until he groaned and she pressed her lips to his shoulder and together they cried out the climax of their union to the silent house.

They lay together for some minutes while the last flame flickered and died. Livvy could not think. She was simply aware of him panting, sweating, moaning, his salty skin male against her mouth. It was magical, lying like that. How she had needed him and needed him still, covering her with his own strength; hiding her from the chill air; saving her; making love with her.

Love . . . The word itself shimmered like a flame and then died. He had lain like this, after all, just hours since, with Sonia. 'You', he had said to Sonia, looking into her eyes. 'You and only you.'

'Me?' Livvy whispered pleadingly under her breath. 'Me and only me . . . ?'

He took his weight on his elbows and raised his head. 'What?' he growled softly.

What have you done to me? she wanted to cry, but didn't. She had wanted it done, after all. There could be no doubt of that. And she had known that he wanted her because he had told her time and again. But he had also told her that he wanted her only when she could be mature about being wanted—and being had.

'Nothing,' she replied, and gave a false smile.

He eased away from her, peering into her face, silent.
His eyes dazzled her. She closed her own eyes and
turned her head away.

He dragged himself into a sitting position, wriggling
as he tugged his jeans up under the male curve of his
buttocks. She watched through nearly closed eyes.
Gluteus maximus, she told herself. That is what that
muscle is called. It is used for making the leg work, hence
its power and strength. Then she opened her dark green
eyes very wide. How terribly mature I am to distance
myself from the sight of his hips like this, she thought.

'Livvy?'

'Yes?'

He was looking at her again now as she lay limp upon
the carpet. But he wasn't looking into her eyes, nor mur-
muring sweet nothings into her ears. He was looking
down at her naked body and frowning a perplexed frown
and smiling a taut smile. A bit like studying the sweet
trolley after you've eaten pudding blindfold, she thought.
What exactly was it that he'd just consumed and did the
appearance match the flavour...?

But when he did meet her eyes he looked almost appalled. 'There's blood...' he said roughly. Then he added,
'I thought you felt ... different somehow. That was your
first time, wasn't it?'

She nodded very maturely. 'Yes. I'm sorry. I'm not
experienced like your other women.' Then, infuriatingly,
big, childish tears welled in her eyes and tipped over on
to her cheeks. 'I don't know why I started it. I don't
know what came over me,' she babbled stupidly, fighting
to regain her non-existent poise. 'I was so frightened—
and so relieved to be alive. Thank you.' She sniffed hard,
her chin puckering.

He went on staring at her. 'Oh, dear. I feel such a
fool, crying,' she muttered apologetically, sitting up on

the prickly carpet, her thighs clamped modestly together and her knees bent. She used one hand to cover her swollen breasts while the other struggled to reach her discarded T-shirt.

He knelt beside her and almost disdainfully picked it up and dropped it in her lap. 'Here you are,' he said quietly.

She searched out his eyes and held them for a fraught moment. His face was completely without expression now, but none the less she was sure that the fixity of his gaze was intented to chasten.

Oh, dear. She wasn't being at all mature. He was no longer looking at her like a man who had tasted a delicious dessert, but like a vegetarian who had been unwittingly tricked into eating meat. 'I'm sorry,' she said again, her voice shaking. 'I really don't know why I acted like that. Please understand... I was so frightened. Still, it's not a problem, is it? Just one of those things. It couldn't be helped, could it? It was an...extraordinary situation. We both could have been killed.'

He looked away from her then as if he couldn't bear to see her. With his back to her he stood up and fastened his trousers. There was the makings of a dark bruise on his shoulder—presumably from his daredevil dive over the couch—overlaid with the red weals of her fingernails, and she desperately yearned to jump to her feet and soothe it with those same fingertips that had marked him, but of course it was out of the question.

He seemed to sense her eyes burning into his back, though, because he suddenly spun around, snatched the T-shirt from her fumbling fingers, rolled it into a ball and threw it on the floor, muttering, 'It's a bit late for modesty, Livvy.' He loomed over her. Jerkily, he scooped her up in his arms and crashed out of the room with her and up the stairs. She was intensely conscious of his bare chest, of the sensation of her cheek pressed against it, and of her own shaming nudity. She was also conscious of an irrational, tremulous and undoubtedly infantile excitement shivering inside her. Was he going to take her to bed? Was he going to make love with her again? She peeped up at the angle of his jaw, and seemed to feel a great rush of love as she watched his face. 'Leon?' she whispered.

'Not now,' he muttered roughly. 'We'll talk later.'

Wounded, she closed her eyes. He carried her to his room and laid her on his big bed. Then abruptly, to her dismay, he left the room. A few minutes later he came back with a glass of water and a couple of pills.

'What are those?' she asked, rolling on to her stomach and letting her tangled hair fall forward to shield her face.

'Only antihistamines,' he said. 'I keep them in case of insect bites, but they also make you drowsy. You've had a very nasty shock. You'll be better for a good sleep.'

'I don't think——'

'Take them,' he ordered sharply.

Anxiously she sat up and swallowed the pills. Then he went into the bathroom where she heard the rush of water. When he returned it was to find her struggling into his robe. He waited until she had belted it and then came and gingerly took hold of her upper arm. 'I'm going to help you take a bath. Now, don't complain. You're too shaky to manage alone.'

Once she was sitting in the warm water his large hands gathered up her hair and twisted it deftly into a knot. 'Don't get it wet,' he commanded. 'It'll take too long to dry, especially as the hairdrier only works in the kitchen. The rest of the house still has round pin plugs.'

Livvy bit her lip. Everything he said made it worse—more obvious that she had not provided the sort of casual sex he had had in mind. For instance, how did he know how long it would take her hair to dry? Leon had undoubtedly waited impatiently for many, many of his lovers to dry their hair. He probably knew better than she did how long it would take. But at least he had been prepared to wait for *them*. At least he had looked into *their* eyes and murmured sweet nothings.

And then he picked up a big sponge and began to soap her back. She looked down at her body, pale beneath the water. There were several bruises emerging where the force of his passion had kneaded her soft flesh against the hard floor. Her breasts looked fuller than usual, the nipples flushed and hard with wanting him. She looked up at him and tried a lopsided smile. But he stiffened slightly and looked away.

She looked at him again, but his eyes were busy watching his hands soap her back and he didn't—or wouldn't—meet her eye. It was only the fear of crying again that kept the tears from her eyes.

'I think the tablets are beginning to take effect,' she said huskily at last. 'If you'll leave me I'll get out now and get dried.'

He handed her the sponge and straightened up. 'OK. I'll put out something for you to wear on my bed,' he said.

She frowned uncertainly. 'It's all right. I can sleep in my own bed.'

But he shook his head and at long, long last he did give her a smile. It wasn't one of his dazzling smiles. It was half-hearted and tired, but it was at least intended to reassure. 'Sleep in mine,' he said, sighing. 'It's more comfortable, and you'll have a functioning bathroom on hand in case you feel ill.'

Meekly she acquiesced. Tucked up in his huge bed, all alone, with the early evening sunshine streaming though the crack in the curtains, she began to weep. It had been her first time. She wasn't a virgin any more. And it had been extraordinary and wonderful and while it was happening, at least, she had lost herself so deeply in Leon that if she hadn't known better—and of course she did know better—she would have believed herself in love with him. And yet now, just an hour later, she had been discarded like so much torn packaging. At which thought the tears flowed even more swiftly until at last she cried herself to sleep.

It was Sunday. Somewhere in the distance she heard church bells ringing. Leadenly she got out of bed and padded to the bathroom. Her eyes looked puffy and bruised, her nose still pink after the bout of weeping. Determinedly she stuck her chin in the air and walked straight out of the bathroom, into the corridor and along to her own room. When she got there she almost wept again. Her bed was tousled but empty. Leon had slept in it, and when she put her face on the pillow, as she felt stupidly compelled to do, she could smell him. She glimpsed herself in the mirror, gathered the pillow into a solid lump and threw it across the room. Then she pulled on a T-shirt and jeans, tugged a brush through her hair, which still smelt faintly of woodsmoke and was unpleasantly fuzzy after the drenching it had received on the beach, urged enough cold water out of the basin taps to splash her face and clean her teeth, and then went boldly down to his kitchen.

He was sitting at the ultra-white table, sipping coffee and frowning. He didn't look at her when she came in.

'Leon?'

He glanced briefly at her and then looked away.

'Oh. I see. You haven't had breakfast yet?' she bit out. 'Well, excellent. In that case I can say exactly what I want to say without fear of interruption. First, I intend to use your kitchen and bathroom. The whole idea of trying to live like an eighteenth-century peasant never made any sense to me anyhow. After all, Rosamund would have been used to the lifestyle of her own age and class just as I'm used to my own modern-day lifestyle. Such things wouldn't have been hardships to her. And if I'm not bowled over by your fast car and country clubs, then I think it's perfectly safe to assume that Rosamund wasn't tempted by porcelain and silk.'

'How about my body? Weren't you bowled over by that?' he asked sarcastically.

'No.' She glared at him. 'As I said yesterday, it was a unique situation.'

'So it hasn't changed your mind about anything?'

'No. After all, it wouldn't have happened to Rosamund.'

'Not even if her husband had saved her life?'

'No,' she returned firmly. 'She would have been wearing eighteenth-century costume which would have been so difficult to remove that she would have come to her senses long before anything like that could have happened. And she would have had eighteenth-century values imprinted in her mind. I don't.'

He eyed her coldly. 'Don't you? Then how can you know how she would have reacted?'

Livvy's face burned with indignation. Oh, dear. She wasn't being very mature, was she? Not like Katya. Not like Sonia. 'Because I have my *own* principles,' she muttered angrily.

'Really? It rather looks to me as if you've jacked in your principles, lock, stock and barrel,' he growled.

'I have not!' she spat. '*You* decided that doing without kitchen and bathroom should be my principles anyway. Not me!'

He eyed her coldly. 'Yes, well...' He sighed, and studied his coffee. 'Actually, you jumped to conclusions. Admittedly, I bundled you out of this kitchen and into the other one because I was annoyed with you, and I have to admit that I did dress it up as a rational decision. But you took it from there. As it happens, I restricted your movements in the house simply because the place has patches where the timbers are rotten. Ironically, your safety was all that really concerned me. Witness the conservatory.'

'You knew it was dangerous?'

'I ought to. I've been in the building trade since I was sixteen.'

'Then why didn't you warn me?'

'Now funnily enough that's exactly what I spent most of yesterday evening asking myself. To be honest, it didn't occur to me that you'd go into the conservatory. There was a couch in front of the door after all, and I'd told you not to go into my room. I hadn't counted on your being so... unprincipled, though.'

Livvy's face flamed. 'Unprincipled? Me? Considering the way you carry on with women I think you've got an incredible nerve. At least I have the excuse that I was frightened to death and very grateful to you for rescuing me. You were still warm from Sonia's bed, not to mention cheating on Katya for the second time in twenty-four hours.'

He flashed her a look of unremitting scorn, getting quickly to his feet. 'I've had enough,' he said nastily. Then he crashed out of the kitchen without a backward glance.

She stuck out her tongue at his receding figure, but as she watched him go she was assailed by another of those great bolts of love which had been attacking her heart since the previous afternoon. Fraudulent bolts of love. Because she did not love him. She merely found him overpoweringly attractive—physically. She was deceiving herself because she couldn't face up to the humiliation of having betrayed her principles. She was conning herself. That was all...

When she went into her sitting-room it was to find that her new kettle had been fitted with a round pin plug, and her work had been rescued from the wreckage of the conservatory and placed on her table. The paper was cut to ribbons. She rubbed absently at one of her bruises and struggled with the weight of her love.

She couldn't bear it. She was listening for every tiny sound, every creak and groan of the old timbers which might signal his arrival. She wanted to be near him, and she couldn't help herself, and it was driving her round the bend.

In the end she gave in to temptation and went to his kitchen to see if he was there. He wasn't. She switched on his kettle and tried to shake some of his coffee granules into two of his mugs. But she lost her nerve. How did he get it exactly right? She opened the cutlery drawer and absently rummaged for a teaspoon. And then she frowned and peered hard into the drawer. The cutlery tray was an old wooden one, and had shifted slightly as she had stirred through the jumble of knives and forks and spoons. And where it once stood there was now revealed the faint, dingy outline of its former position. This cutlery drawer hadn't been cleaned out for months and months...

Leaving the automatic kettle to switch itself off, she ran upstairs to his bathroom and examined the grouting around the tiles. And the shelves of the wall-mounted cabinet. And the tarnished copper pipes behind the basin's pedestal.

There could be no doubt about it. Both the kitchen and the bathroom had been in place for several years. Not weeks...

Livvy cringed with embarrassment. She slowly made her way downstairs to face the necessary task of apologising to the man with whom she appeared to be genuinely falling in love.

But, although his car was parked out front, of Leon there was no sign. She went out into the garden and tried to enjoy sunning herself. But she couldn't get Leon out of her mind. She kept remembering how it had been to make love with him, and sharp tears kept stinging her eyes. She slumped in one of the chairs, sighing.

'There you are...'

It was him, dressed in his tennis whites again and carrying his racket. He dropped it carelessly on the grass and came to sit opposite her.

'Leon,' she said anxiously. 'I want to apologise.'

'Don't,' he bit back so fiercely that she was stunned.

'But——'

'But nothing. Let's stop raking over old sores, huh?'

'But I've just found out that you didn't have the kitchen installed.'

He looked at her very drily. Then he slowly raised one eyebrow. 'I know,' he said.

'Well, of course you know, but I just wanted to apologise——'

'And I've already told you not to bother.'

'All right.' She looked away so that he wouldn't see the hurt in her eyes. But looking away proved not to be enough. She got to her feet.

'Sit down.'

'I've got things to do.'

'You have nothing to do more important than listening to me. So sit down.'

She perched uncertainly on the edge of her chair. 'Can't you leave me alone to get on with my work?' she muttered.

He tilted back in his chair, studying her coldly with his hooded eyes. 'If I'd left you alone yesterday afternoon to get on with your work, God alone knows what would have happened.' There was a pause. 'Or wouldn't have happened.'

'Yes. Well.' Livvy's face burned. Then she burst out defensively, 'The thing is, it was your fault in the first place. If you'd told me that the house wasn't safe I wouldn't have gone near the conservatory. And don't tell me that it was my own fault for jumping to conclusions, because you've deliberately misled me about the house. You told me that you were the one who'd had the kitchen and bathroom installed when it was the Foxes all along.'

'I didn't tell you any such thing, Olivia. As it happened, that was another conclusion you jumped to.'

'But you didn't contradict me. You deliberately let me go on believing that you'd——'

'Trashed the place?'

'Oh. OK. Have it your own way. Yes, I suppose I did say that. But you encouraged me. All that stuff about crowbars and lump hammers and ripping the place to pieces was designed to lead me even further up the garden path, wasn't it? And because I thought that all the building work you had in mind was more of the same it never occurred to me that the house was unsafe. You risked my life.'

'Yes.'

'Yes? Is that all you have to say?'

'I apologise unreservedly.'

'Oh.'

'Is that acceptable? I can assure you that I am not happy with the way things have turned out. Not at all.'

Well, terrific. That was just the sort of thing a woman needed to hear from the lips of the man who had made love with her for the very first time not twenty-four hours since. 'You should have told me the truth,' she scowled.

'And so,' he said freezingly, 'should you. Livvy, you should have told me that you were a virgin.'

'It was none of your business.'

He gazed at her appalled. 'It became my business. Once it was apparent what was going to happen...you should have said then...'

She looked at the floor, her heart thumping. He wouldn't have made love with her had he known. 'I'm sorry,' she lied.

'Now, perhaps we can stop squabbling and you can start listening. You pointed out a couple of days ago that our behaviour was puerile. I am more than ready to agree. So might I suggest that we adopt a more mature approach while I take you around the house as I intended to do the moment you arrived and show you the trouble spots in order to avoid further catastrophes? However, I must point out that it was only the conservatory which was in imminent danger of collapse. Everything else is reasonably sound.'

Did making love with her count as a catastrophe...? A horrible ache buzzed behind her eyes. 'Am I supposed to be comforted by that knowledge? Or should I even believe it?' she returned bitterly.

He closed his eyes and one corner of his mouth puckered with contempt. 'Livvy, you always believe exactly what you choose to believe. If you really think that I'm about to let you walk on floors that might give way beneath you at any moment then you're a bigger fool than even I imagined.'

Oh, why had she been such an idiot as to get mixed up with him? Even now her heart was melting at the sight of him and he loathed her! She'd practically begged him to make love with her and yet all he'd ever done was insult her. How had she got herself into such a position? 'What do you mean by that?' she asked leadenly.

He shrugged. 'If I were in your shoes and I didn't believe what I was being told about the condition of the house I'd leave.'

'Is that an invitation? Do you want me to leave?' she bit out accusingly.

'No,' he said evenly, then stood up and stretched. 'Are you coming or are you going?'

'Lead the way,' she sighed. 'I'll follow.'

CHAPTER TEN

'PURTEN END has both dry and wet rot in certain timbers. And woodworm,' said Leon calmly, leading the way indoors. 'It's going to have to be more or less taken to pieces and put back together again. When it comes to the final appearance of the place—well, it will depend to an extent on what exactly we uncover during the renovations, but essentially it will all be put back into as authentic a condition as possible. There will be modernisations, but nothing irrevocable or obtrusive. Now, in this room here there's wet rot in the floorboards over in this corner. You could jab a screwdriver through it, but that's all. You couldn't jab your foot through it, for instance. And the plaster is loose on the ceiling above, but again, it's not a very big patch and it's not in such a poor condition that it might fall on your head.'

The guided tour continued, with Livvy listening in silence to his explanations of what exactly was wrong and would need doing. Leon clearly knew exactly what he intended to do with the building, and Livvy could do nothing but gawp at his shoulders in mounting dismay. He understood old buildings. He was sensitive and knowledgeable about old buildings. He cared for them. Perhaps he even loved them. Livvy didn't want to hear all this.

'And that's about it,' he said finally, slapping hands dusty from pulling free a loose piece of plaster on the seat of his shorts.

'*Gluteus maximus*,' she mumbled resolutely under her breath, her gaze transfixed.

'What was that?'

'Nothing. You obviously know exactly what you're doing.'

There was a cold little silence. Then he turned and gave her a cold little smile. 'Surprised, Livvy?'

'Why didn't you tell me sooner?'

'I didn't want to spoil your fun.'

She was silent for a moment. 'I suppose I did rather jump to conclusions.'

'*Did rather*? Livvy, you do nothing but.'

'Well, OK. But bear in mind the fact that the first thing I ever saw you do was cut down a mature, healthy tree.'

'A sycamore. They grow quite quickly, actually. And it was felled for a wood-turner. It will eventually end up as furniture.'

'Oh. Oh, I see... Well, there was the footpath. I knew about that before I ever spoke to you as well.'

'I fenced off the footpath because there's a rare wild orchid in the woods beyond. I needed to offer it some protection until it had set seed and I didn't have the time to go about it in any other way. However, I concede that strictly speaking I commited an illegal act by obstructing a public right of way.'

Livvy looked down at her hands. 'I... How was I supposed to know that? You didn't tell me.'

'I didn't know whether or not you were a wild-flower collector at that point. I had good reason for not telling you.'

She glared at him accusingly. 'Did I look like one?'

'What do they look like? Do they walk around with sacks on their shoulders marked "Floral Swag"? Don't be absurd, Livvy. Anyway, by the time the question arose I didn't feel like justifying myself in your eyes. You had already gone out of your way to be offensive to me.'

'So what are you trying to tell me? That you're the world's greatest conservationist?'

'I do my bit.'

'Oh, yes!' she exclaimed scornfully. 'Your bit! And you also put up ugly great skyscrapers all over the place.'

'What makes you think that?'

'Your building firm!'

'My firm specialises in houses. We also do a lot of restoration work on ancient buildings. Believe it or not we are considered specialists in our field.'

'But I came into your office,' she protested vehemently. 'I saw the model!'

'That model is of a 1950s office building in downtown Chicago. It won prizes in its day, and is, in fact, quite a classic of its kind. Anyway, the good people of Chicago believe that it contributes something to their historic skyline so are employing us to deal with some problems it has developed due to the use of faulty pre-stressed concrete.'

Livvy closed her eyes. She really didn't want to look at his muscles now. 'I don't suppose you're really planning to tear Richard Gallagher's firm to pieces either, are you?'

'No.'

'Nor throw people on the unemployment scrap heap?'

Leon sighed heavily, and pressed his lips firmly together before he spoke. 'Ironically,' he began, 'Richard often uses a lot of stonemasons—because of the type of work Gallagher's has always done—but he's always had to lay them off between contracts before now. They'll be a great asset to Roche and Son. The restoration work we tender for should see them in full employment well into the next century.' He shrugged. 'As to the rest of them—well, the construction industry has its ups and downs. Short-term contracts are the norm—"job and finish'', they call it. In fact, people often work in the building trade because they like the challenge of frequent job changes. But I doubt any of Gallagher's people will fare worse after the merger, probably a lot better. Because of our restoration expertise—which is a pan-European venture and less subject to the whims of the market—we aren't as vulnerable as most building firms.'

Livvy swallowed. 'I'm sorry,' she said leadenly. 'I got a lot of things wrong, didn't I?'

One corner of his mouth curled sardonically. 'Don't apologise, Livvy,' he jeered. 'Getting things wrong is your forte after all. You're a specialist in your own right. Hold your head high. Be proud.'

One corner of her mouth puckered with dismay, but she managed to bring it under control. 'I expect you're right about my book, too.' She sighed miserably.

He studied her for a long moment. Then he folded his arms. 'Do you mean that, Livvy?'

'Maybe.'

His scrutiny intensified. She glanced away.

'Well, come on. Make up your mind,' he demanded impatiently.

Livvy shrugged. 'I'm still thinking about it.'

And then he threw back his head and laughed. 'Don't tell me that you're ready to admit it's trash, after all?'

'Not quite,' she returned shakily. 'But I expect it's only a question of time.'

'So you do think I'm perfect after all?' he goaded.

'Isn't that what you've been trying to tell me?'

'Good lord, do you seriously want me to answer that? Or have you merely jumped to the conclusion that I'm perfect and you're simply looking to me for confirmation?'

She grimaced. 'You certainly aren't perfect,' she replied scornfully, a little of her usual spirit returning since he had laughed at her. There was always the business of Katya and Sonia after all. Did he honestly think that she wouldn't *mind* about them? 'You've got a lot to learn when it comes to women, for a start,' she added coldly.

Anger flashed in his eyes. But to her surprise he said nothing, though she could tell by the way he'd clamped his lips together that he'd like to.

But she needed to hear the worst. 'Just as a matter of interest, how many women are there in your life at present, Leon? Oh, and don't count me in. I'm married and I'm definitely not willing.'

Still he said nothing.

'Katya and Sonia I already know about,' she continued grimly, determined to spoil things once and for all. She was damned if she was going to carry a torch for this man for the rest of her life. All he had to do was reveal that horrible, barbaric side of himself again and she'd be able to put out of her mind forever this stupid business of loving him. 'What about your secretary, Gina? She didn't strike me as being the brainiest secretary in the world. On the other hand, she's a very pretty secretary. You could have any secretary you want, after all—brains and beauty combined—but perhaps you're more interested in the fatal combination of single and willing... Is Lulu single, Leon?'

She'd gone way too far. Wrath was stamped across his face, black ire seethed in the pupils of his cold blue eyes. She felt a flash of fear. But still he said nothing.

'Well...?' she persisted determinedly, fearful of his countenance but still anxious to drive matters to the bitter end.

'Do you want to call it a day, Livvy?' he asked freezingly at last.

'You mean you want me to stop asking about your girlfriends?'

'No. That wasn't what I meant.'

'You mean us...the marriage...'

'Yes.'

She blinked twice, very slowly, before she dared trust her voice. 'I...I... Yes. But we can't.'

'We can do anything we want to do.'

'We've only been married for a matter of days.'

'So? I've been known to do more unconventional things than divorce after a three-day marriage.'

'Well, bully for you!' she snapped back, her wounds making her aggressive. 'However, you were the one who deceived my parents. You were the one who sold them a pack of lies and made all their dreams come true by putting them on the QE2 for a fortnight. So you can damn well put up with me for a decent interval of time. There's no way I could explain to them why love at first sight disappeared after just *three days*. And if I tell them the truth it'll break their hearts. *And* sully their memories of their holiday. *And* make them feel used. So you're stuck with me for six months. It'll seem then as if we gave it a proper try but it just wasn't to be.'

And then Livvy looked at him and her heart ached for him, barbarian or not, and she shouted wildly at him, 'Do you think I want to stay here now? Do you think I can bear it? You don't know how awful it is for me! But I'm not going to hurt them and that's that. So you can just stuff it, Leon bloody Roche! You've had what you wanted and now you can damn well pay for it! Business principles, OK? You see, I learn fast...'

'I've had what I wanted?' he echoed incredulously.

'You've had me!' she flashed back, and then turned on her heel and stormed towards the staircase, desperately trying to hold back the tears which were scalding her eyes.

But he was behind her in a moment. She sensed him a hundred times more strongly than she had the previous day when he had crept up upon her in the conservatory. She felt as if she knew every inch of him now—and she couldn't tolerate his nearness. It was bad enough that she'd told him how she felt, without falling into his arms and showing him as well! She began to sprint, taking the stairs two at a time.

He halted abruptly halfway up the stairs, and when she risked a glance from the safety of the landing he was standing very still, his hands on his hips, looking up at her, his face livid with anger. 'Livvy,' he commanded in a taut, controlled voice. 'Come back. We need to talk this one out.'

'No!' she replied, her back to him, but the single word had given her away. Her voice had been thick with tears, and to her horror her shoulders began to quake and a sob tickled the back of her throat. Oh, lord . . . he would come now and comfort her. And she would give everything away . . . Panic-stricken, she raced ahead to her room.

But he hadn't wanted to comfort her after all. Because although the sobs shook out noisily as she stumbled to her room he didn't follow.

He did come knocking around two. He said in a steady, consoling voice, 'I've had lunch sent over from the club. It's set out in the garden. Come now or it'll get cold.'

And, of course, she came. Even though it made her feel sick to hear the pity in his voice.

He was waiting for her on the landing. She'd tidied up her face, had put on some make-up and had even coaxed enough water out of her taps to wash her hair.

She smiled weakly at him. 'It's very kind of you to organise a meal. But really there's no need. I could have——'

'Could have boiled an egg over a camp fire,' he said drily. 'I know.' And then he met her eyes and held her gaze and said, 'Livvy, let's try the mature approach again, huh?'

She nodded, swallowing hard and running her fingers through her damp hair.

'Come on, then.' He smiled, dazzling her as usual, and took her arm very, very gently, as if she were an invalid. 'Let's go and eat.'

Livvy was humiliated beyond measure. If she had any sense at all she would walk out of Purten End and drive off into the sunset. But whatever sense she might once have had had evaporated in the heat of her passion. She was mesmerised by Leon. He hated her and yet she was still eager to waft in his wake, out into the garden, to sip wine with him and to see if she could perhaps, even at this late stage, redeem herself just a little in his eyes. Because she was still fooling herself that she loved him. And people in love, it seemed, had no sense at all.

There was a leg of lamb, waiting to be carved. And roast potatoes and beautifully cooked vegetables and a bottle of wine.

Livvy sat down primly on the old wrought-iron seat and smiled wanly at Leon. 'We've made a real mess of things so far, haven't we?' she said balefully.

He nodded silently, taking a large knife into his beautiful hand and pressing the steel blade gently against the meat.

'You see, when I agreed to marry you I intended to stick to my ideals. I wanted to prove to you that it was possible to live in a way that wasn't dictated by business principles,' she said ruefully.

He concentrated on carving the meat, saying nothing.

'I didn't make much of a success of it, did I?'

One corner of his mouth tightened, and he slanted a curious glance at her but he kept his own counsel.

'But the thing is, Leon... Oh, if only you hadn't played that stupid game of pretending you were completely black-hearted... Well, the thing is...' But just looking at him had made her forget what it was that she wanted to say.

His muscles tightened in a faint hint of a shrug. She felt the sun warm on her face, and when she touched her hand to her hair it was almost dry and felt silky beneath her fingers. Good. Perhaps if her hair shone and she smiled a lot and... Oh, damn it. She was loosing her marbles now...

'Is it really traditional in your family to give a brooch instead of a ring?' she asked nervously.

'No.'

'Why did Sir Richard know that there wouldn't be a ring in that case?'

'I once had an argument with him about the symbolic nature of wedding-rings.'

Oh, dear. Did that mean that he didn't believe in marriage? 'I...I suppose you were making it up about Richard Gallagher's insisting that you had a wife, too?' she blurted out brightly.

'No.'

'Really?'

'Yes.'

'You mean he really did insist on that before he'd sell the firm to you?'

'He did.'

'Oh.' Oh, dear. She'd been rather relying on that... After all, it seemed very improbable that Sir Richard would have stipulated such an extraordinary thing to a

businessman like Leon who did pan-European restoration work and everything... She had rather hoped there
might have been another reason why he had tricked her
into marrying him... But then, if he didn't even believe
in marriage...

'Don't you believe in marriage?' she asked weakly.

'I don't believe that white dresses and rings make a
marriage,' he responded laconically.

He laid several slices of lamb on her plate with the
flat blade of the knife. 'Enough?'

'Oh. Yes. Shall I help myself to vegetables?'

It was a delicious meal. Livvy forced herself to eat
though the food kept turning to sawdust in her mouth.
They were being mature and civilised, sitting here making
small talk, and Leon seemed to be enjoying it as far as
one could tell, and she'd be a fool to stir things up again.

'How big are the gardens here?'

'About ten hectares.'

'Oh. This is a lovely place to sit out.'

'Uh-huh.' His mouth chewed and sipped and
swallowed. Sunlight caught the moistness of his lower
lip and gilded it.

She was still tempted. Dreadfully tempted. And all
she wanted now was to tempt him in return. Which was
ironic, because he certainly didn't want to tempt her any
longer.

They were still sitting at the table sipping when the
sound of a car engine disturbed their peace. 'Now who
can that be?' Leon asked.

Livvy shrugged. 'No one for me. No one knows I'm
here.'

Leon made a dismissive gesture with his eyebrows and
leaned back in his seat.

'I'll go round to the front,' Livvy said uneasily, half
getting up from her chair.

But Leon reached out a hand to stay her. 'If whoever it is wants to speak to us then they'll have to wait.'

'It might be burglars.'

'Unlikely.'

'Yes. Even so...'

He shook his head. 'Stay put.'

Livvy took in a deep breath. He wanted her to stay. He wanted to be with her in the sun-filled garden all alone. Unconsciously she beamed at him.

'Happy, Livvy?'

'Uh...it's a lovely day.'

'It's been a lovely day for a couple of weeks now. This is a marvellous summer.'

'Uh...yes. What a shame my parents are missing it. I mean, I know they'll be having nice weather too, but the thing is, we get so few real heatwaves like this in Britain and...um... Well. Let's hope it lasts till they get back.'

One eyebrow quirked and he studied her carefully. 'Why don't they approve of your being an illustrator, Livvy? I don't understand that. Most parents would be delighted at the way your career has gone.'

'It's not the fact that I'm an illustrator that disturbs them,' Livvy began cautiously. She nibbled at the corner of her mouth. 'They think it's too...too lonely a life for me, working on my own all the time. They would have been happier if I'd gone to work for an advertising agency or a newspaper or something.' Somewhere, she added silently, where I might have been meeting potential husbands. Somewhere with Christmas parties and dinner dances and staff restaurants. Somewhere where I might have used my talents to catch a man like Leon Roche. 'They...um...they don't understand that I enjoy my work for its own sake. When they were young they didn't have the chance to pick or choose their own careers, you see. They just worked hard at whatever came to hand, and made a success of it without worrying whether or not it gave them job satisfaction. They don't realise that it's different for me.'

'I see.' Then he asked, 'Do you think you would have been so determined to do your own thing if they'd been more understanding?'

Livvy looked at him, perplexed. 'You mean am I simply reacting against them and the way they are? No. I'm sure I'm not. Actually, we've always got on well despite our differences. I don't think my ambitions have anything to do with them. It's just the way I am.' And then she stopped speaking and a huge involuntary sigh juddered past her lips. Oh, listen to the man! Why couldn't he have spoken to her like that the very first time they met? Why did he have to wait until now before showing an interest in her? Now was far too late.

Somewhere within the depths of the house the doorbell rang. 'Hadn't one of us better go and see...?' Livvy murmured.

But Leon shook his head. He didn't say anything.

'Suppose it's...um...a telegram?'

He shrugged. 'They phone telegrams through these days.'

'Oh, yes. I forgot.'

Livvy's stomach was beginning to somersault under his scrutiny. She looked down at her jeans and pleated the edge of her enormous white T-shirt with its motif of jungle animals and its plea to save the rainforests and wished that she'd worn her blue and white striped sundress. She pulled a face. Now she really had taken leave of her senses, hadn't she?

'What's the matter?' he asked sharply.

'Nothing,' she mumbled.

'Jumping to conclusions again, Livvy?'

She forced her mossy-green eyes to meet his steadily. 'No.'

There was another uncomfortable silence. And then came the sound of the car engine starting up and driving away.

He gave no sign that he had heard it. Which could only mean that he wanted to talk to her more than he wanted to answer the door. It was a start, of sorts...

'Does your father really live in a tax haven?' she asked meekly.

'No. He lives in the States—the country which nurtured him and educated him and all that other stuff you said. He's an American by birth. He came over here with the forces, and stayed to marry my mother. She's Polish originally. She left the Warsaw ghetto when she was a child...'

'They sound like very extraordinary parents.'

He shrugged. 'They were very odd parents. My mother was always brim-full of emotion which she discharged by playing the violin—badly—in the bathroom for hours on end. My father was a carpenter and set up a building firm. He was something of an expert simply because wood is used far more in construction in America than it is here. Consequently he developed an expertise in renewing timbers in old buildings. It was steady, consistent work. But he wasn't ambitious and I think he found the business of making a living burdensome. Though he loved my mother and us kids, and was a good father.'

'Us kids'? She dared not ask whether one of them was Katya... Instead she asked, 'How do they like life in America?'

'They love it. Dad's enjoying retirement, and Mum saws away at the catgut with some oddball string quartet and they appear to have all they want in life now that she's able to devote herself to her art.'

Livvy sighed. So there it all was. Pat. The story of his life. A story which added up to his hating artists. Hating people who were dedicated to creativity. Hating the kind of romantic love which made a dupe of men. Hating *her* really. Everything about her. No wonder he thought her story was trash.

'Us kids'... She took a deep breath and then lost her nerve. 'Is there anything else you'd like to put the record straight about, Leon?' she asked. 'I mean, are there any other conclusions I've jumped to which need ironing out?'

There was a horrible pause. And then he said very deliberately, 'No.'

He stretched and got to his feet. 'Now if you'll excuse me, I have to go and get washed and changed. I've got to drive back up to London. I've got a meeting, and I'm due to pick up Lulu at eight. I don't want to keep her waiting.'

'A meeting? On Sunday evening?'

'Yes. We're rebuilding a ruined *Schloss* in Saxony. There are problems. I'll have to fly out to Germany first thing tomorrow.'

'How long will you be gone?'

There was a studied pause. 'I don't know,' he said, and then he turned and went back into the house.

She watched the white cotton of his shorts tighten across his buttocks as he shoved his hands into his pockets. She watched his calf muscles hardening with every step he took. 'Gastrocnemius and soleus combining to form the Achilles tendon,' she chanted under her breath... She looked up at his big, hunched shoulders and the golden sun bouncing off his glossy black curls before he disappeared in through the gaping kitchen door, and her heart wept.

In the depths of the shrubbery a dark bird fluttered. He had deceived her. And he had tempted her. And now she had succumbed and there was no way back. Silently, helplessly, she waited until she heard his car driving away.

It took precisely three days for her to discover exactly how far he had been deceiving her. The firm of landscapers who turned up to convert the old grass tennis court into an orchard explained that the old trees had been destroyed by something called honey fungus. What a bit of luck, the foreman commented, that Mr Roche had been able to swap sites.

A brand-new Mini Cooper was delivered, midnight-blue with a border of guelder-roses.

Katya rang to ask where they had been on Sunday afternoon when she had driven all the way from London to meet her new sister-in-law. She was surprised to learn that they hadn't been expecting her—until she realised that the children—whom her ex-husband had taken to the zoo on Sunday—had been playing with the bedroom extension and must have cut her off.

Then Sonia rang. 'Tell him I've organised the timber he wanted for Llanfihangel castle.'

'Pardon?'

'The yew. You know... He was adamant that it had to be yew, although I tried to talk him into using oak. Why did I bother? He always gets his own way. Oh, and tell him that I've figured out how to protect the bats and the owls during the restoration work. I'll get the report to him in a couple of days.'

'Bats and owls?'

She laughed. 'He sat up all night with my infra-red cameras, watching them. I've seen similar sights hundreds of times, but it was his first time and he was quite transfixed. I left him to it in the end. It was freezing out in those stables in the middle of the night.'

'Yew and only yew...' muttered Livvy dispiritedly, adding, 'Thanks, Sonia. I'll pass the message on.'

When she rang Gina to pass the message on the switchboard operator apologised, but explained that Mr Roche's secretary was in the loo. 'Ring back in ten minutes,' she sighed. 'She ought to be back at her desk by then. Honestly, she spends half her life in the Ladies', fixing her make-up. I don't know why Mr Roche puts up with her.' And then the woman paused and added apologetically, 'Except it's hard for a single mum trying to earn a living, isn't it? You've got to make allowances, if only for the kiddy's sake. At least, that's what Mr Roche says.'

Lulu. Loo-loo.

A carver-up. A destroyer of people's lives. A trasher... Or a man who tolerated a barely competent secretary for the sake of a child? Did it matter? Whatever he was really like, it scarcely mattered. Because he couldn't care less what Livvy thought of him. And anyhow, she was beginning to suspect that even if all her worst suspicions had been true it would have made no difference. It wouldn't have changed her feelings one bit. She went straight up to her bedroom for a good cry.

He didn't come back through all the next week. Nor the next. Builders arrived to clear the wreck of the conservatory and began work on removing some of the ancient WCs. Livvy's period started. And curt notes turned up in the post concerning the building work. She read and re-read his unruly black script. 'Allow them access to... Provide them with facilities for... On no account should they...' She even sniffed the paper and thought she could smell something male and woody about the heavy notepaper. But even if she could, it wasn't the same.

Livvy threw herself into her work. She used the morning for her artwork when she was fresh and the rest of the day she spent searching the library. Major Fox had replied to her letter at last, saying that he thought he'd put the papers between the pages of a largish book to stop it getting dirty. Livvy carefully took out each largish book in turn and eased it open, taking great care neither to damage the spine nor to introduce dust between the pages. Then she went through all the smallish books. And the lumber-rooms and the cupboards and the chests of drawers.

She even found the trunk full of old corsets, and gingerly took them out to examine them. Mostly they were utilitarian 1930s originals in a faded pink, complete with nasty, dangly old metal suspenders and mysterious buckles and bits of tape. Ugh ... But there was one, the cambric brown with age, the bones bent, which she was sure was of Rosamund's era. She went into Hereford and checked in the library and measured and copied and made patterns and cut and stitched.

But although she could keep her hands and her head busy from dawn till dusk, her heart dawdled disconsolately, even in the dead of night. It wanted him. It wanted to be with him. It wanted to hear his voice and see his beautiful face and be loved by him in return. Oh, foolish, foolish heart.

It was small consolation that Livvy's artwork was taking on a new intensity as a consequence: that Rosamund on the page came to wear Livvy's heart on her sleeve, and even spoke, when Livvy came to revise the text, with Livvy's heart in her mouth. Her work was so important to her that she ought to have been pleased, except that her work didn't, after all, seem to be quite so important to her any more.

He came on a wet summer's day in the middle of the week, wearing a dark suit and a white shirt and a tie as blue as his eyes. He was tanned an even deeper brown and he spent a lot of time crouched down with one of the craftsmen examining the floorboards in the hall. Livvy knew because she kept walking past on vital errands, hoping he'd turn his head towards her and smile a dazzling smile and say hello.

In the end, sick of herself, she returned to the library and glared at book-spines and tried not to listen for his footfall. But she heard it none the less. He walked up behind her and her heart thundered so hard she thought she might collapse. She kept her face turned to the books. He came and stood at her shoulder, saying, as usual, absolutely nothing. Her hand began to shake. Briskly she ran her fingers through her hair, turning slowly to face him. 'Don't tell me you haven't had breakfast yet?' she said in a brittle voice.

'Come into the kitchen. I want to talk with you. We'll be more private there.'

'Right.' She felt herself blush crimson and tucked in her chin so that her eyes were fixed on the crisp white shirt covering his abdomen. She could see the wall of muscle moving in and out as he breathed. Oh, dear. Now, what *were* they called? The vertical muscles were the superficial ones and...and... She looked up again. 'Why are you here?'

'The panelling in the hall is going to have to come off and I wanted to be here to discuss it with the craftsmen. But more importantly I needed to see you.'

'Oh.' She wanted to be pleased by what he had just said. It sounded so promising... And yet she couldn't let herself feel pleased because she didn't want to be disappointed.

As it happened, her caution didn't protect her from disappointment. The moment she had nodded her assent he turned his back on her and began to saunter off, and, there being no choice, she followed. In the kitchen he took off his suit jacket, stretched, loosened his tie and undid the collar button of his shirt, stretched again and then filled the white jug kettle and shook some coffee granules into two mugs. Then he turned to her, smiled a serious, non-dazzling smile and said, 'How are you, Livvy?'

'Me? I'm all right.'

He frowned. 'It struck me that we made love without using protection. Are you *sure* you're all right?'

Disappointment ballooned in her stomach like warm dough. 'Yes. You've nothing to worry about there, Leon,' she said, her voice tight and hard and small.

He shrugged. And *then* he gave her the dazzling smile she'd been hoping for. It was a smile of relief. He poured boiling water into the mugs and added a splash of milk. 'Sit down,' he said, dropping into one of the chairs and nodding at her.

She sat.

'How are you getting on?'

'Fine. But I haven't found the story yet.'

'What will happen if you can't find the document?'

'Well, so far it isn't a problem. I'm still managing to get a lot of useful work done.'

'But you can't finish without it?'

'Um . . .' She narrowed her eyes and chewed worriedly on the corner of her mouth. Would he expect her to leave if she couldn't find the document after exhausting all the possibilities? She couldn't even bear to think of it. While she was here at Purten End she was able to live in hope that he would turn up at any moment and make love with her again. Of course, she wasn't such a fool as to think it was likely. And nor was she fool enough even to think it desirable, because she knew quite well that were it to happen she would be hurt even more in the long run because he didn't even like her. But in the short term it would be analgesic, and her pain was already grave enough to have blurred her vision. 'There are still plenty of places I haven't looked,' she returned defensively.

'What happens when you've looked everywhere?'

'I...uh... Look, I'll cross that bridge when I come to it, all right? The thing is, at the moment my work's going well. The solitude here is ideal.'

'I thought you felt that it was such a special story that you had to be absolutely true to it in every detail?'

She coloured slightly and looked out of the window. Indeed, she had said exactly that and had meant every word of it at the time. But in truth the story was beginning to take on a life of its own. 'Mmm...' she agreed vaguely.

'How would you feel if I began living here at weekends?'

'I...Leon, it's your house. And we do have an agreement. Of course you must spend as much time here as you want.'

He tilted back in his chair, laced his fingers at the back of his neck and surveyed her with hooded eyes. He breathed in and held his breath so that his chest swelled beneath the fine cotton of his shirt and held it taut. One corner of his mouth hinted at a smile.

And then the phone rang.

'I'll take it in the hall,' he said.

Livvy looked at the space where he had been, feeling very, very empty. She got up and went to sit in Leon's seat, still warm from him, and still with his jacket draped carelessly over the back. Warm and male and woody and terribly, terribly real was the air she gulped into her lungs. She would never love anyone in the way that she loved Leon. She had known it when she'd married him. Known it really, in a funny sort of way, when she'd first set eyes on him. It hadn't exactly been love at first sight— but whatever it was it had been unique. She loved only Leon, and without him there was nothing. And worse than nothing, she reminded herself bleakly, with him.

CHAPTER ELEVEN

LEON took to coming down at weekends. He would arrive on Friday night and leave on Monday morning. He could easily have come on Saturday and left on Sunday, and Livvy tried hard not to be pleased. After all, this was his home. He was bound to want to spend time here. And there were the renovations to supervise.

They never squabbled. In fact, they were unutterably polite to each other. Leon would ask after her work, and she would make a few non-committal comments and then he would ask after the house, and she would tell him of any problems the craftsmen had encountered. Sometimes they would pace the grounds together, and discuss which shrubs needed pruning, and whether a parterre would look good below the terraces. He would take her to the country club to dine, and she would study the menu while he studied the wine list. She made a point of never eating the same things as he did. She always envied him his choice.

One September evening, when they were strolling around the ornamental lake, Livvy remarking on the pond weed, and Leon speculating about water lilies, Livvy suddenly got a fit of the giggles. 'What is it?' Leon asked.

'It's just...' She smothered a grin. 'Well, you know those gardening programmes on television?'

'I don't watch TV.' And then very politely he added, 'But do tell me all the same.'

'Oh. Well, it's just that they often show an expert wandering around a beautiful garden like this with the

174

owner. And it's just ... well, their conversations put me in mind of us.'

'Which of us is which?' he quizzed civilly.

'Oh ... You're the owner, of course,' she replied.

'And you're the expert?' he responded drily.

'No!' Livvy coloured. 'No...' she continued tentatively. 'I used to think I was an expert on all sorts of things. I know better now.'

Leon stared very hard at her. 'I'm sorry,' he said, and though he said it softly he said it importantly, as if it was meant to mean something.

Livvy very maturely bit her lip and looked away. 'Sorry for what?' she queried softly.

But he didn't reply. He just wandered off to examine some chrysanthemums. And Livvy was glad because it gave her a moment to compose herself. He rarely refused to reply these days, and when he did it reminded her too strongly of those heady days when neither of them had been at all polite.

That night when they walked over to the country club there was a chill in the air. Livvy folded her arms across her chest, cuddling the heavy cotton of her white and silver batik trouser suit close against her skin and wishing she'd worn something warmer. Even Leon, who, she had observed, wore suits as little as possible, preferring loose, casual clothes, had donned a jersey with his denim shirt and jeans.

'You're cold,' he observed, and he pulled off his sweater and offered it to her.

'No!' she exclaimed nervously. 'I'm all right. Really. It's just a bit autumnal but I like it.'

He thrust the sweater closer to her. 'Take it,' he repeated.

She glanced at him in panic, but did as she was bid. It would have been too obvious not to. But oh, it was awful putting it on. It was warm from him. It smelt of him. She almost choked with desire.

'I promised to take you to the Solomon Islands in September,' he said evenly.

'Oh, I didn't take that as a promise, for goodness' sake,' she replied. 'After all, when you said it you were... I mean, I believed then that I had to be a proper wife in public for the sake of your business and our agreement and everything and that we had to put on a show of having a honeymoon. But since Sir Richard... I mean... You know, it hasn't needed to be like that after all, has it?'

'Sir Richard is still on the board. He's not planning to stand down at the end of the six months.'

'Oh.' Livvy winced. 'You mean he still isn't convinced?'

'No.'

Livvy frowned. 'But Leon, he seemed a very nice man when I met him. And you're a very... well, you aren't what I thought you were. So what's the problem?'

Leon shrugged, stuffing his hands in the pockets of his jeans. The chill air had made all the dark hairs on his arms stand on end. 'The problem is that Sir Richard doesn't have an heir. He and my father both started out in a very small way and were good friends. They often worked together. They've known each other for a long time.'

Livvy gasped. 'Don't tell me that you want me to have a baby! Oh, Leon...'

'Livvy!' he exclaimed, sounding absolutely delighted. 'Livvy, you just jumped to a conclusion!'

'Oh, shut up.'

'But it's wonderful. I tried to goad you into jumping to conclusions when you found out that I'd tricked you and you went all mournful on me. But you wouldn't. I thought you'd never do it again!'

'I said shut up.'

When she glanced at him he was grinning broadly.

'OK. Don't shut up,' she muttered. 'After all, it was only because you kept shutting up that I kept jumping to conclusions. Just tell me the truth. I mean, why is Sir Richard uneasy? And why is he so adamant that you have to be married?'

Leon laughed. And then he said, 'He's known me all my life. He refers to me as the renegade of the building trade. I have to admit that I've always done things my own way—rarely toed the line. I mean, for years I refused to wear a suit and I wouldn't do anything that smacked of what he calls ''settling down''. Well, he has a few minor health problems these days—nothing much, but it reached the point where he wanted to take things easier than his business would allow. I offered to buy him out. But he remembers my teenage self too clearly. He said he'd be delighted to sell to me once I was married—not before.'

'Hence the marriage.'

Leon didn't reply.

'So you want me to take a honeymoon in the Solomon Islands with you for the sake of Sir Richard's health? So he'll retire properly?'

But Leon shook his head. 'The old boy's welcome to stay on the board for as long as he likes. He's getting the best of all worlds at present. And I *never* do anything I don't want to do, Livvy.'

Like marrying me . . . ? she wondered.

'You mean you actually *want* to take me away on holiday?'

'Yes. Though I wouldn't expect it to be a honeymoon.'

She sucked in a huge breath. 'Oh, dear. No. I'm sorry, Leon. It's out of the question. I mean, I have my work to do and time's running out and my publisher's getting sniffy and... Well, the things is, I don't really think we should.'

'I won't tempt you again,' he said grimly. 'That's a promise.'

Ow! He'd really meant that... She shook her head. 'I believe you,' she said weakly, unable even to contemplate the temptation such a holiday would afford. 'It's not that. It's... it's my work... the document.'

'Livvy, you've had nearly three months in which to find that document. I've put off having the library cleared for as long as possible, but I can't delay it any longer.'

'I... well, that doesn't matter in itself,' she prattled frantically. 'I mean you can clear the library but it won't make any difference to me. Because I've searched the library from top to bottom. It clearly isn't in there. And there are three rooms finished now in which I can work so I don't need to work in the library at all. But there are still lots of places I haven't looked. Hundreds. All the attics for instance...'

To which he sighed but said nothing.

And that proved to be that. Leon commented on the blackberries in the hedgerow, and Livvy fingered the welt of his sweater and commented on the weather. Dinner was excellent. Her own salmon seemed a little dry, but Leon's soufflé looked impeccable, and the wine he selected was, of course, just right.

Livvy found it harder than usual to sleep that night. He wanted to take her to the Solomon Islands? Not for any reason but just because he wanted to... But then again, he was going to have the library cleared—her excuse for being there was about to be snatched away...

Should she have turned him down? But if she went, what then . . . ? The thing was, if he was interested in her at all, then why couldn't he be interested in her here at Purten End? And if he was interested in her then surely he'd let her know. Leon was no shrinking violet, after all. So what did it all mean . . . ?

At three a.m. she gave up on sleep and went down to the library. She unlocked her work from the drawer where she kept it at weekends and spread it out on the big central table. It was almost done. There was still a good deal of detail to complete, but each illustration had taken shape. Each word of the text had been refined until it read so tenderly, so beautifully, that it brought tears even to Livvy's eyes. She still had research to do, but research that would be better done in the university library in London. And she had long ago given up all hope of finding the document—and anyway, she no longer cared. She had no excuse for being here. Not any more.

She traced the outline of an illuminated capital with the tip of one finger, tears welling in her eyes. And then she froze. The skin prickled on the back of her neck. He was in the room with her. She knew it beyond a shadow of a doubt. He was silently padding up behind her, and she was frightened.

'Livvy? Couldn't you sleep?'

She heaved out a sigh of relief and turned to face him. His hair was tousled, his chin dark, his brow gold in the lamplight. He was wearing a white towelling robe and nothing else as far as she could tell. But what he looked like, for once, didn't matter.

He had stopped six or seven feet away from her. She was, fortunately, between him and her work. She rested her hands on the table behind her, spreading her arms as wide as she could manage without actually drawing attention to the fact that she was shielding the pictures from his sight. Please don't let him try to look at them, she prayed silently. She'd die if he did...

'Oh, hello, Leon. No. Couldn't you sleep either?'

'No.'

'Shall I get you a warm drink?'

He said nothing. His eyes were dark. She couldn't see the blue of them for once.

'A hot toddy? There's plenty of milk in the fridge.'

Still he said nothing.

'I'll just put these away,' she added, trying to sound natural as she swiftly turned, her white linen nightgown billowing as she moved. Her trembling fingers scrabbled wildly at the papers.

'Stop,' he commanded.

She went on trying to make an orderly pile but her fingers were shaking too much.

'Livvy,' he said insistently and he took a couple of paces and clamped his hands to her shoulders. 'What's the matter? You'll damage your work if you handle it like that. Look, just because I'm having the library cleared it doesn't mean you have to give up on the book entirely! For God's sake, you said yourself that the document wasn't in here. So just stop it. You'll tear them.' And his voice was low and fierce and very, very intense.

He turned her towards him, and to her relief he studied her eyes, ignoring the untidy pile she had made of her artwork.

She was shivering. 'I'm going to go back to Bristol,' she said resolutely. 'I... actually, there's no point in my staying here any longer.'

His fingers dug hard into her shoulders. 'But just earlier you said there were still lots of places... the attics...'

'I know. But I really don't believe it's here. The major treasured that document. He thought it was important enough to show me when I was fourteen. He wouldn't have stuffed it away in a dusty old attic. I'll go. It doesn't matter.'

He pushed her a little further away from him, the better to scan her eyes, and he said roughly, 'Don't go, Livvy. Not yet.'

'But . . .' Her mouth was dry. Her entire body seemed to be on fire.

'Please, Livvy. Not until . . .' For once he was the one to sound uncertain, and then he said resolutely, 'Let me make love with you before you make any decisions about your work. Please.'

'What?' Her lips felt papery as she closed her mouth.

'Let me make love to you, Livvy.'

She took in a huge breath. 'Why? Just this evening you said that if we went to the Solomon Islands you'd promise . . . I mean . . . Look, I don't understand.'

'But you aren't coming to the Solomon Islands, are you? You're going to go away and you're never going to be the same person again. Because of me. I've destroyed all your fine ideals, and I can't bear it. I've waited and waited for things to come right with you, and I can't wait any longer. Livvy, it's kill or cure.'

She swallowed hard. 'Kill or cure?' she croaked.

'Livvy, I imposed my set of values on you, and I . . . I crushed you. But if you let me make love with you one more time I will show you that it can be good. That it needn't be destructive. That there is something to salvage after all, and that we were both right in our own ways.'

'I don't understand,' she muttered painfully.

'Look, I used to believe that sex was just a carnal thing—that marriage was just a way of legitimising it. I always said that I'd never bother with that bit of paper—if I was committed to a woman and she was committed to me, then all the trappings wouldn't matter. That's what I used to believe, Livvy.' His eyes burned into hers. 'But *you* believed in something quite different. Something honest and true according to your own light. And I took it away from you when I made love with you that once.'

He swallowed hard, and there was a pause as if he was waiting for her to say something. But she couldn't speak.

'You made a mockery of all my beliefs, Livvy,' he said huskily, and it couldn't be true but his eyes seemed to brighten and blacken before he blinked them back to blue. 'Because I didn't even give you the carnal pleasure that I once claimed it was all about. And quite frankly, although I took my pleasure, that wasn't *all* it meant to me. Not by a long shot.'

Still she said nothing. She just watched his eyes, knowing that very word he spoke came from his very human heart.

'I was so fast—so fierce—so certain that a woman as beautiful and spirited as you would have been loved to distraction time and again and would know how to find her own satisfaction...' He paused and blew out a leaden breath. 'And I was so... Well, I just did what came naturally. I couldn't seem to hold myself back.'

There was a long silence. A silence in which Livvy tried to say that indeed she had taken her pleasure in full measure. But she couldn't bring herself to say the words. Because if she told him that then ... Ah, then he wouldn't want to make love with her again...

'Let me make love with you one more time,' he insisted. 'Let me do it slowly and patiently. Let me— what is that bit in the marriage service? The church service? You know. ''With my body I thee worship...''?

Yes. Let me worship you with my body, Livvy. Let me show you how wonderful it can be. So that you can take something worth having out of all this.'

To which plea she simply laid her cheek acquiescently against his breast. He gathered her to him. He swept her into his arms. And once he had taken her to his big bed he unbuttoned her high-necked Victorian nightgown and worshipped her with his body. Very slowly. Very patiently. Very lovingly. And she worshipped him in return.

When dawn broke, they were still entwined in each other's arms. Leon's powerful, hair-roughened thigh lay like a blanket across her golden skin. Her auburn hair was strewn across the pillows, her mossy-green eyes open to soak in every glimspe of him she was to be allowed before she had to go away.

She hadn't intended to fall asleep at all. But the steady rise and fall of his chest, the regular thump of his heart against her ear, must have lulled her.

And when she awoke he had gone. Still she lingered. There were crumbs here to be gathered. The scent of him on the sheets—the sense of his presence on the warm stretch of bed beside her. She closed her eyes and soaked him in, hoping most fervently that he would come back and worship her once again, and she could tell him that she was ready to throw all her principles to the wind if he would just let her stay with him and be committed to him, because she no longer cared that he didn't love her because she loved him so and she'd never, ever be able to live without him now.

'Livvy?' He was bursting through the door, wearing just his jeans. He was scowling furiously. And he had her illustrations in his hands. 'For crying out loud, Livvy!' he roared, thrusting them towards her.

She eased herself up on her elbows, pulling the covers up to her chin.

'Why the hell...?' He gritted his teeth, cast the illustrations angrily on to the bed and demanded, 'What does it mean?'

'I...I thought the hero would look better with dark hair,' she stuttered. 'Rosamund is blonde and it made a better contrast.'

'Dark hair?' he returned incredulously.

'Well, yes. I...um... It was a bit difficult to change the eyes from blue, though. So I kept them.'

'I know you said you were just interested in my muscles from an anatomical point of view,' he said explosively, 'but I didn't believe you! Is that all I am to you? A life model? Well, damn it, Livvy, if you try to publish this I shall sue. I promise. That man is me, and you had no right to put me in your book like that.'

'I...I couldn't seem to help myself,' she admitted soulfully. 'I...um... The drawings just started to come out that way and I couldn't...um... Well, the thing is——'

'The thing is,' he continued furiously, 'you've made me into a sex object.'

'Sex? You must be crazy! There's only one chaste kiss in the whole book.'

'Ha! There don't have to be any kisses for sexual infatuation to be present. It's there on the page, Livvy. Deny it if you can.'

'Well...um...the thing is...'

'And the *story*, Livvy. This is a beautiful, wonderful love story. It has to be based on personal experience— and fairly recent experience at that, because you damn well didn't have a hap'orth of experience when I met you. But it's *nothing* like the original.'

'It is! That first draft you saw . . . I'd got it wrong. I . . . um . . . I kept remembering bits and I realised I'd got it wrong and——'

'And in that case you need to see a doctor. There's something seriously wrong with your memory. Because in the original document it says—I mean it actually states—that Rosamund only consents to marry him because she wishes to be a fine lady.'

'That can't be true. I don't remember that . . .'

'And there's absolutely nothing in the original about her falling in love with him at first sight. Well, in fact she actually goes on to say that she does not care for him but she is a poor girl and she has often been hungry and she will be his wife and will eat his food and warm herself at his fire and wear his fine raiment, but he can only look at her from afar and then——'

'Leon, *none* of that was in my first draft. Where on earth did you get the idea that all that was part of the story?'

He scowled at her. 'Because I have the wretched document locked up in my briefcase. As I said from the outset, it's a simple story of lust and avarice.'

Oblivious to her nakedness, Livvy knelt up, throwing her shoulders back, her eyes blazing. 'In your briefcase? And exactly how long has it been there?'

'I went looking for it on the day you first came here. As the major said, it was between the pages of a largish book.'

'Damn you to hell, Leon Roche. Why did you keep it hidden? How could you let me go on and on looking for it when you knew perfectly well it wasn't there?'

'Because you wouldn't have liked what you saw. It would have wrecked your ideals. And anyway, you would have gone away once you'd seen it,' he growled back. 'And I wasn't about to let you do that!'

'Why not? You hated me!'

'Don't be so bloody stupid. I took one look at you and I decided you were the only woman in the world for me. I could hardly have hated you, now could I...?'

'Huh! Oh, brilliant! Love at first sight, eh?'

'Well, with the benefit of hindsight, yes, it probably was. Because I sure as hell love you now and I can't remember a time when I didn't...'

Livvy clenched her fists. 'Love me? You have behaved abominably towards me. You don't know the meaning of the word. You starved me and kept me short of water and you tried to make me live like an eighteenth-century peasant girl and you...you even wanted me to believe that you had a bunch of single and willing women on a string.'

'Yes. Well.' He stroked his stomach with the tips of his fingers and then rumpled his curls. 'Look, I wanted to make you feel jealous, OK? I mean, you wouldn't admit to yourself, let alone me, that you fancied me. I figured that if I made you jealous you'd have to face up to your own feelings. After all, how was I supposed to make you fall in love with me if you wouldn't even talk to me? That first day you just wanted to run away as fast as your legs would carry you even though it was so obvious that there were sparks flying between us. What would you have done if you were me?'

'You were unscrupulous,' she accused. 'You told my parents a pack of lies.'

'Every damned word I told your parents was the truth,' he boomed. 'And, let me tell you, there was no way in the world that they were ever going to be hurt after six months because we *are* going to live happily ever after and that's that.'

'Happily ever after? You and me?' she yelled incredulously.

And then he flung himself on top of her, forced her back on the bed and, putting his face close to hers, growled angrily, 'What do you think last night was all about, Livvy? Can you live without me? Because I'm damned sure I can't live without you.' And with that he wriggled the long brown fingers of one hand into the back pocket of his jeans and produced a wide gold band.

'Give me your left hand,' he commanded.

'What for?'

'For the wedding-ring.'

She clenched her fists and beat them feebly against his shoulders. 'No fear!'

'Oh, come on! I've always said that people shouldn't wear wedding-rings until they've lived together for a while and they're sure they can put up with each other for the rest of their lives. Now give me your hand and let me put it on you!'

She squirmed out from under him and sat up, glaring at him. 'So you want me to make *your* story come true now, do you?' she asked, running her long fingers through her tangled mane of hair.

'Yep.'

'No chance. I'm not letting that ring on my finger until I've bought one for you. If I'm going to promise to put up with *you* for the rest of my life then you can darned well do the same for me.'

He laughed then, pulling her down beside him. 'OK,' he said, dazzling her with his smile. 'We'll go shopping next week. And we'll have a church wedding with all the trimmings and all the vows.'

'For my parents? For Katya?'

'No. Just for us.' And then he put her fingers to his lips and kissed them very tenderly. 'I'm sorry I spoiled your wedding night, Livvy,' he murmured.

She frowned. But she didn't say a word.

'You know, you said a marriage was made on the wedding night... We can never be null and void now, even though I got it wrong first time.'

'We had our wedding night in the afternoon.' She sighed smugly. 'To the accompaniment of breaking glass. Isn't there some country where they break glasses at weddings? For luck, or something? Anyway, it certainly brought me good luck. And it was everything I could ever have dreamed of. It was when I fell in love with you, Leon.'

He kissed her very slowly. Then he broke away and said, 'And it didn't matter that I didn't satisfy you?'

'But you did,' she admitted ruefully.

'In which case, Livvy, you weren't telling the truth when you said——'

'Oh, shut up, Leon.'

And he did. Dazzlingly.

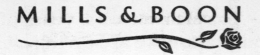

MILLS & BOON

Next Month's Romances

Each month you can choose from a wide variety of romance with Mills & Boon. Below are the new titles to look out for next month.

THE SHINING OF LOVE	Emma Darcy
A BRIEF ENCOUNTER	Catherine George
SECRET OBSESSION	Charlotte Lamb
A VERY SECRET AFFAIR	Miranda Lee
DEAREST LOVE	Betty Neels
THE WEDDING EFFECT	Sophie Weston
UNWELCOME INVADER	Angela Devine
UNTOUCHED	Sandra Field
THIEF OF HEARTS	Natalie Fox
FIRE AND SPICE	Karen van der Zee
JUNGLE FEVER	Jennifer Taylor
BEYOND ALL REASON	Cathy Williams
FOREVER ISN'T LONG ENOUGH	Val Daniels
TRIUMPH OF LOVE	Barbara McMahon
IRRESISTIBLE ATTRACTION	Alison Kelly
FREE TO LOVE	Alison York

To celebrate 10 years of Temptation we are giving away a host of tempting prizes...

10 prizes of FREE Temptation Books for a whole year

— **plus** —

10 runner up prizes of *Thorntons* delicious Temptations Chocolates

Enter our Temptation Wordsearch Quiz Today and Win!

10th All you have to do is complete the wordsearch puzzle below and send it to us by 31 May 1995.

The first 10 correct entries drawn from the bag will each win 12 month's free supply of exciting Temptation books (4 books every month with a total annual value of around £100).

The second 10 correct entries drawn will each win a 200g box of *Thorntons* Temptations chocolates.

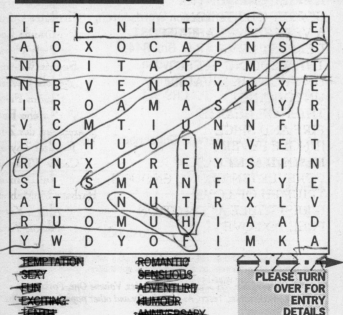

I	F	G	N	I	T	I	C	X	E
A	O	X	O	C	A	I	N	S	S
N	O	I	T	A	T	P	M	E	T
N	B	V	E	N	R	Y	N	X	E
I	R	O	A	M	A	S	N	Y	R
V	C	M	T	I	U	N	F	U	U
E	O	H	U	O	T	M	V	E	T
R	N	X	U	R	E	N	Y	S	N
S	L	S	M	A	N	T	F	L	E
A	T	O	N	U	T	R	X	L	V
R	U	O	M	U	H	I	A	A	D
Y	W	D	Y	O	F	I	M	K	A

TEMPTATION
SEXY
FUN
EXCITING
TENTH

ROMANTIC
SENSUOUS
ADVENTURE
HUMOUR
ANNIVERSARY

PLEASE TURN OVER FOR ENTRY DETAILS

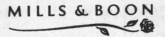

MILLS & BOON

HOW TO ENTER

10¢ All the words listed overleaf below the wordsearch puzzle, are hidden in the grid. You can find them by reading the letters forward, backwards, up and down, or diagonally. When you find a word, circle it or put a line through it.

Don't forget to fill in your name and address in the space below then put this page in an envelope and post it today (you don't need a stamp). Closing date 31st May 1995.

Temptation Wordsearch,
FREEPOST,
P.O. Box 344,
Croydon,
Surrey
CR9 9EL

COMP395

Are you a Reader Service Subscriber?   Yes ☐   No ☐

Ms/Mrs/Miss/Mr _____

Address _____

_____

_____ Postcode _____

One application per household. You may be mailed with other offers from other reputable companies as a result of this application.
Please tick box if you would prefer
not to share in these opportunities.   ☐